THE GUARDS OF TELARI
By
Derrick J. Truesdale

**To Shawn, Christina, Jamir, Kareem, and
Kennedy**
Telari is Home, always protect our home!

If you want to go fast, go alone. If you want to go far, go together.

— African Proverb

PROLOGUE

TELARI, AN EARTH derivative planet, one of many planets spread across the various galaxies. The planet is smaller, roughly one third the size of Earth but has proportionate land masses which outnumber the bodies of water.

The planet, similar to its' big sister, has manufactured housing, a stabilized government, commerce, and a multitude of mixed cultures and animal life spread out across the planet.

Unlike Earth though, there is no interstate system, no airlines to speak of, no travel by vehicles except horse drawn carriages unless you are driving a hover vehicle for the purposes of delivery of necessities to shop keepers or governmental outpost.

Businesses are few and they are only for the manufacturing of items needed for the people of Telari to live.

Healthcare is managed collectively and there are health centers strategically placed around the planet for the most effective benefit of the people.

The governing council of elders make the decisions which ensure that the habitants of the planet are well cared for and taken care of.

In remote areas around the planet, there are astrological outpost with astronomers watching the sky in order to alarm the inhabitants of potential problems or threats.

There are warriors on the planet, but there is no structured or organized militia, something that the elder council, against advice from the galactic space council, did away with decades before.

Advanced technology for travel was also done away with, also ill advised.

It was nighttime on the planet. The air was warm and breezy, and other than a few musical sounds from the nocturnal wildlife, it was rather quiet outside.

A hooded woman traveled alone to one of the nearby villages with an infant in her arms.

The infant, with beautiful brown skin and bright eyes, cooed and cawed as she looked up smilingly at the woman.

The woman put the baby on the front step of a domicile unit and knocked twice on the door.

As the door started to open, the woman took three steps backwards.

A woman stuck her head out the door.

"Hello?" she inquired as she looked from side to side and saw nothing.

The cooing of the baby caused her to look down as a look of slight shock grew on her face.

"Oh my...," started the woman as she quickly bent over and picked the infant up off the ground.

"ABE!" she called as she turned around and took the baby inside.

"What is this?" asked Abe as the woman walked towards him, gently holding the baby in her arms.

"Oh Abe," she started as she smiled and unwrapped the baby from the blanket. "It's a gift from the Trinity, I'm certain of it! She's a gift from the Trinity!"

"Was there a note or anything?" he asked checking the blanket.

"No," she started as she moved over to the sink and started running some water, checking the temperature with her fingers. "No note! Just this little bundle of joy."

The woman, Sarah, was past her prime. Though she never had any children of her own, she always wanted one, specifically, a girl.

He joined her at the sink and put his finger in the baby's hand and smiled.

"I guess us old fogies can be good parents," he said smilingly.

The baby appeared to smile back at him.

"What's this?" he asked as he looked at the wrist of her right hand.

"I guess it's a birth mark," she said as she started wiping the baby off in the sink.

"A birthmark?" he asked. "There is a perfect circle with a triangle and an eyeball in it?"

"Well as I said, a gift from the Trinity. You know how I've always wanted a baby."

He studied the baby and then smiled.

"Yeah, she's a cutie!"

Sarah pointed in the direction of the room.

"Get me one of those cloths," she said, "from off the chair back."

Abe complied.

"We don't want to drop any surprises," she said in a baby voice as the baby giggled a bit.

"Wow Sarah," he started as he returned quickly with the cloth. "It's almost as if she understood you."

Sarah laughed. "Don't be ridiculous, she's just a baby."

She wrapped the cloth around the baby's bottom as a diaper and then wrapped her back up in the blanket.

"Well what are you going to name her?" he asked.

She held the baby out in front of her and stared as the baby smiled back at her smilingly.

"I think I'll name her...Christina," she said. "Oh I can tell just by looking at her, she is going to be special someday!"

***

Five years later, Christina was outside playing in the dirt with her friend Steven who appeared to be levitating rocks in his hand as she watched smilingly.

"That's very good Steve," she said. "I can see something under them as you lift them, you just have to think about what you want them to do as you do it."

Steve moved his hand over and the little rocks followed.

The rocks then fell to the ground.

"How did you know that?" asked Steve.

"I'm not sure about that," started Christina, but I did see something. She then looked up towards the sky with concern.

Sarah came out of the domicile unit. "Christina, you and Steven come on in here for some lunch."

The two kids quickly got up.

"Your mom would be upset with me if I didn't feed you and put you down for a nap," she said to Steve as he smiled and the kids went into the home.

Upon hearing a loud whistling sound, she turned around and looked up and saw what looked like multiple flying crafts flying across the sky.

She quickly and nervously closed the door.

"ABE!" she called as he was just giving lunch to the children.

"There's some flying things in the sky," she said.

"What?" he asked, "we didn't get any notifications of any attacks?"

Loud whistling sounds erupted as laser fire could be heard outside the home.

"Come on kids," started Abe as he held his hand towards the children and signaled them to follow him as Sarah ran over to a door and opened it.

They all ran inside and down some steps as Abe locked the door before joining them in the darkened basement.

They all huddled together as they listened to the chaos above.

***

As the laser fire erupted throughout the bazaar, Mark and Justice each picked up one of the twins and started running for what looked like a storage shed but just as they turned a corner, a demon looking creature grabbed Justice violently, causing her to drop her son as she screamed.

"MARK!...Alex!" she yelled while pointing and being hauled off.

Alex ran quickly to his dad who put him inside the shed with his sister Nicole.

"Stay right here til I get back!" he said just before quickly closing the door and going after the creature who took his wife.

Alex peeked through a hole in the door and watched as his father jumped the alien who took his wife.

He saw his mother fall to the ground as more aliens grabbed his father and started pulling him off.

He then saw his mother get up off the ground and attempt to run to them as another alien jumped on her, knocking her down.

Alex gasped.

"They got mommy and daddy!" he cried.

Nicole growled and kicked down the door and ran towards her mother.

Justice mouthed the words, *Nicole NO!!*

Nicole yanked the alien by his back and threw him off of her mother as two more aliens approached.

She stepped hard on the toe of one of them and then punched him in the crotch.

Another one reached for her, and she bit his hand causing him to scream and she then punched him in the face, knocking him out.

Justice looked behind her and saw more aliens coming towards them. She then turned around and looked at Alex.

"Alex," she started sounding fatigued, "please get your sister out of here!"

He nodded and grabbed his sisters, hand and took off, running so fast that her feet stayed off the ground.

They soon ended up in an area dense with trees and far from the alien activity as Alex let go of her hand.

Nicole looked around.

"Why did you do that?" she asked as she struck him and caused him to fly backwards into a tree.

He fell unconscious.

Nicole gasped as she covered her mouth.

"ALEX NO!" she yelled as she ran over to him and tried to sit him up by placing an arm behind his head.

"I'm sorry, I'm sorry," she cried.

***

"DADDY? MOMMY?" called young Kevin as he moved through the secluded wooded area by himself unaware that there were aliens moving towards him, looking for more Telarians.

A bird screeched from high above, causing Kevin to look up.

All of a sudden, he heard a loud pant and a growl behind him, and he turned around just in time to see a large black panther running towards him.

Scared, he turned around and started running and then he fell just as he saw the aliens reaching for him.

The large black panther jumped over Kevin and aimed himself towards the first alien's chest landing directly on him as the alien growled.

The large panther then bit down on the aliens' head, hard, causing his body to go limp.

The other aliens turned their attention to the panther but too late as it moved quickly and dispensed with them just as quickly as he did with the first one, while the child watched.

The panther then roared as he turned his attention to young Kevin wo was laying on the ground watching the whole time.

The panther moved slowly towards the young boy while growling.

The large cat was within inches of the small child as Kevin looked up nervously.

"Get up on my back," said the panther.

"Huh?" asked Kevin.

"I need to get you somewhere safe," said the black panther.

Kevin was shocked that he was able to understand the black panther but was happy he wasn't trying to eat him. He quickly got up and climbed onto the panther's back, and it took off further into the woods.

***

The council of elders locked themselves in the council building and cowered in the corner as they heard the screams of the other Telarians outside when suddenly a blast came through a wall and some of the aliens entered holding weapons aimed at the group.

Then another alien walked in, significantly larger than the others. He moved close to one of the council members and smiled, while the member whimpered nervously while looking away.

We never should have done away with the militia! He thought. *We never should have forsaken our technology, we proved nothing.*

"My lord," started one of the smaller aliens, "Do you want us to put them on board with the rest?"

"No," he said with a deep monstrous voice, "We have enough to get us through to the other systems, we can leave this planet be for the time being."

The elder sighed with relief.

Desatyr, the larger alien, sniffed the man. "Human," he grinned. "I love humans!" He bit the guy's right arm off at the elbow as the man screamed. He then proceeded to hold it and eat it as if it were a large drumstick.

He moved towards the hole in the wall, preparing to leave as he ate.

"There's lunch boys," he started, "be at the ship in thirty!"

The aliens smiled and licked their chops as the elders quivered in fear.

They then dove into the elders and wildly started eating them as they screamed until death claimed them.

The council of elders was no more.

CHAPTER ONE

TELARI RESTED QUIETLY in its solar system sixteen years after its last attack. The world that at first glance feels unmistakably Earthlike, until the eye adjusts.

Roughly one-third the size of Earth, the planet's smaller mass gives everything a subtle lightness: gravity is gentler, movement slightly freer, and even storms seem to roll rather than rage.

The most striking feature of Telari is its sky. Chlorophyll exists naturally in the atmosphere, suspended in microscopic concentrations that filter sunlight throughout the day. As a result, daylight arrives beneath a soft green sky, pale and luminous rather than harsh.

Clouds drift through it like washed ivory and jade, and shadows on the ground carry a faint emerald tint.

At dawn and dusk, the sky deepens into layered greens, mint, sage, and moss, before darkening into a cooler, clearer night.

Telari possesses vast forests and wide agricultural fields, broken up by low mountain ranges rather than towering peaks.

With the exception of Mount Sinovia, these mountains rose gently, weathered and old, their slopes thick with vegetation and stone worn smooth by time.

Oceans cover small portions of the planet, their waters darker than Earth's, reflecting the green of the sky and appearing almost teal from above. Coastlines were calm and fertile, supporting fishing communities and trade villages.

Telarian civilization favors simplicity and proximity to nature. Towns are not sprawling cities but small villages, each separated by stretches of forest, farmland, or meadow. No settlement felt isolated, yet none dominated the land.

Homes here were functional and modest, built from local materials, stone, hardened wood, plant composites, and mineral-rich clay packed tight.

The architecture emphasized durability and climate harmony rather than ornamentation. Structures tended to be low, wide, and open to airflow, with sloped roofs and shaded entrances in order to accommodate Telari's filtered sunlight.

The paths between homes were often unpaved, softened by moss or grass rather than stone.

The villages felt lived-in, not planned, organic clusters shaped by generations based on need rather than by design. Technology existed but blended quietly into daily life, rarely calling attention to itself.

And even though he could run at a speed that was faster than most of the vehicles in possession of the shaytan empire, they were still able to fire upon him.

Alex dodged to the left and then to the right as the wind brushed his face like a cool breeze and as he sensed somehow that another laser was coming in his direction.

Each successive shot seemed to be getting closer and closer to him.

He tried like hell to keep his breathing steady, but with each effort to take a breath, it became increasingly difficult for him to remain focused.

Alex thought he was blessed to have been given the gift of speed but felt it really didn't seem to help him much since one of the aliens had the uncanny ability to disappear and reappear wherever he wanted to, making Alex an easy target.

He soon exited the town and ran into an area which seemed to have been devoid of development by the people of Telari, which it probably was since the inhabitants of the planet have only been there for the last century.

The wooded landscape would make a decent cover for now.

The last time his planet was under attack like this, he and his sister lost their parents, and this only brought back that pain from so long ago, and his current location reminded him of how he ran to the woods with his sister.

The laser fire stopped a few short moments ago, and as he kept running Alex started to smile a little.

He lost them.

He actually did lose them.

His only hope at current was that his sister Nicole was just as lucky as he was if not more.

Alex soon found shelter behind a large redwood and stopped to look behind.

"I am so tired," said Alex as he bent over and inhaled heavily, trying to catch his breath in order to continue until he found help or some sort of shelter. He wasn't sure of where he was going, but knew he definitely had to get there.

The only thing which limited his gift was he got tired and hungry at a rate almost as fast as he could move.

He never learned how to combine his talents with proper breathing techniques and therefore, his gift was not something he could utilize on a regular basis.

"That's it, I can't run anymore," started Alex as he felt as if he were having a difficult time with catching his breath.

"Good you spoiled rotten brat," replied a stranger from behind.

Alex slowly turned around to investigate and saw the familiar face of one of the aliens.

The alien, Gaylor, as called by others, stood at six feet five inches tall and weighed two hundred and thirty pounds, with apparently no signs of extra adipose tissue on his body. He wore a strange military type of uniform, which was Deep red with hunter green accents. If he had been human, he would have been attractive by European standards. He had brown hair, which was neatly combed, and a brown goatee, which was trimmed perfectly. His skin was

Caucasoid, like European humans and appeared to be smooth and flawless.

With the angry look upon his face, his facial appearance was a scary and intimidating one to those who didn't know him. The same fell true for those who did know him.

Alex looked over at the right hand of the space popper and noticed he was holding a mini molecular decomposition canon. He knew the weapon well and saw what it was capable of doing and therefore assumed that that was exactly what it was.

The alien moved closer to the young Telarian and began to admire him for the lack of fear which developed on his face. No matter, he was here to do a job and would do it. "Now you can come with me in peace." He paused as he cocked the weapon. "Or fall to pieces."

CHAPTER TWO

MOST OF TELARI'S animal life mirrors Earth's, mammals, birds, reptiles, insects, but there are minor variations amongst the species as mutations are common.

Some animals possess additional limbs, faint bioluminescent markings, or subtle color shifts tied to the planet's chlorophyll-rich environment. None of these variations are alarming or monstrous; to the people of Telari, they are simply part of the world's natural balance.

Predators exist but are few, and ecosystems remain stable. There is an underlying sense that the planet has reached a long-standing equilibrium, evolution slowed, refined, and settled.

"Thank you, my friend," said Kevin as he lifted his hand and allowed the small black bird to fly off of its temporary perch, his finger.

He also received a gift.

From birth, Kevin had the ability to talk with the animals. Though that may not seem like much, the animals have always been very valuable to him.

They would tell him such information like where to expect rainfalls or dry spells, where to gather the best harvest, and where to find a missing or lost child.

Now they were telling him that the vicious aliens were looking for him and other telarians.

He continued to move through the wooded area as his two-and-four-legged friends continued to inform him of the various positions of what they presumed to have been his enemies.

Orphaned at a very young age, the animals were the only friends and family Kevin had. He had learned by the age of three the importance of good hygiene, but by the age of five, his teachers would teach him a new lesson.

The lesson of how not to depend on adults.

Now at twenty-one years of age, Kevin barely knew how to speak to other telarians, having been devoid of them for over senty-five percent of his life. So now he could only ascertain what was going on, on the planet of Telari by his own observations and what he could gather from his animal friends.

As he moved further along through the forest, Kevin soon located a hidden trap door which he and his animal friends had made long ago in the event there was ever another alien attack.

That day was today.

Kevin opened the door and descended into the ground while closing the door over him. Below ground was the fabrication of a home and it looked like a home except the walls were made of dirt and imprinted with the roots of trees on their surfaces. Even though his eyes had adjusted fast to the world of darkness, he occasionally liked to believe he needed some sort of light and therefore lit a lantern, which immediately brightened the underground cove.

Kevin sat down on a chair he had fashioned out of a tree stump as a small ground hog approached him and climbed up into his lap.

The creature squeaked several times and then waited for a response from Kevin.

"I know," said Kevin as he looked up to the roof of the cove. "But it'll all be over soon, I pray!"

Above ground, the rest of the animals in the wooded area continued to chatter lightly amongst themselves as the aliens soon walked into the wooded area and blindly past the trap door.

After scanning the trees, looking for some of the inhabitants of the planet who may have fled into this area, hoping to escape, One of the shaytans soon turned around to face his troops.

"This areas is clears, head back to the layer!" He barked. The aliens soon left out of the woods.

After being certain that the intruders had left the area, a small squirrel ran over to the trap door and squeaked several times. *Kevin you're safe for now*.

***

The strange aliens spread their reputation around the small planet of Telari very fast via their actions, and as such were known for being ruthless, malevolent and fierce.

Nicole liked them that way because they were easier to fight.

As the aliens gathered up people off of the streets of Humania, Nicole continued to fight valiantly in order to keep the guards from taking her down.

Soon Gaylor, the space popper who had captured her speedy twin brother, appeared standing behind her.

He slowly looked her body up and down and grew enticed by her appearance as her red hair swayed from left to right, yet he was angered by this young woman's ability to resist capture by his troops. *What made her so special?*

He had wondered the same thing about the boy who was able to outrun him and some of his other troops and then wondered how many others on this planet had special abilities and would his master's army potentially have a problem?

His task was to capture all of the inhabitants on the planet in order to provide labor for his master and nourishment for his troops.

Gaylor quickly aimed a small gun at the young woman's back and fired.

A dart hit her in the scapula.

As Nicole swung her fist around in order to hit one of the oncoming aliens, she passed out and into the arms of the creature behind her whom she had never even seen.

"Imbeciles," said Gaylor angrily. He was upset she was so easy to subdue and yet no one else had done it.

He then passed the girl to one of his men,
who then put her over his shoulders and carried
her off.

CHAPTER THREE

THE FIRST BLAST hit the wall beside them.

Heat snapped through the room. Wood splintered. Smoke rolled across the ceiling fast.

Christina flinched, eyes wide, but Steve didn't move, he *couldn't*. He stood with the book raised, jaw clenched, fighting to keep the words from collapsing in his throat.

"From the alabaster sun," he began, voice shaking, "to the moonlit habo trees,"

Shanna stormed in like she owned the air.

She was red-skinned, tall, and built like a hunter who never missed. Her eyes, red, from the orb which was used to control her. She wore a red bathing suit with long matching boots and matching gloves which descended from her antecubital down to her hands, and the gloves were fingerless.

Her hair fell in long brown curls, and her ears, sharp and pointed, cut through the locks like blades.

On her back sat a bow and a quiver filled with arrows.

On her face sat impatience.

"Fire," she commanded, almost bored.

The shaytans unleashed a storm of laser fire.

Steve forced the words out anyway, louder now, desperate.

"Take us away from here and place us..."

Suddenly, time slowed.

A bolt struck the spellbook.

The book jerked in his hands like it was alive.

The pages started flashing symbols, the ink was crawling and twisting, the reality within bending.

Then the book began to slowly dissolve, its edges burning into nothing as the smoke thickened.

Christina coughed, blinking through the heat and the haze.

"STEVE!" she called.

He tried again. He pushed the words out.

"...with the Trinity!"

The motion in the room *stopped*.

Not quieted.

Stopped.

Smoke froze mid-curl. The laser sparks hung in the air like suspended fireflies. The laser glow paused in thin, unmoving lines, as if time itself had been pinned to the wall.

Christina barely caught her breath.

Steve's eyes widened, not with fear, but with recognition, he wasn't fully causing this. Someone else was helping him.

Because his wrist, beneath his sleeve, had begun to burn.

Christina felt her wrist burn too, the pot where her birthmark lie.

The heat along her wrist, sudden and undeniable, like a brand waking up.

Then there was darkness.

The environment changed.

Then a voice filled the room.

Not from a mouth, but from everywhere.

A soft chorus, layered, many voices speaking as one.

"Welcome!"

Christina swallowed hard. "Who...who are you?"

"We are what your people have named, the Trinity."

Steve whispered, barely audible.

"Convergence," he said.

"Yes," replied the voice of Convergence.

The frozen smoke trembled as if it were bowing.

"Neither one of you are not meant to die today."

Christina found her voice. "You've summoned us, why?"

The air swirled and tightened cool around them.

The chorus voice didn't answer with comfort, it answered with certainty.

"Because five beings were threaded, tied at birth. Because the invaders have returned. Because Telari requires protection."

The heat on Christina's wrist flared once.

And the world folded releasing time and the perception of the shaytan attackers.

When the smoke cleared, the book the young Telarian was holding was swirling around in the air where Shanna the huntress last saw him holding it.

The book then started to fall as it slowly vanished as a result from one of the lasers hitting it.

The huntress then smiled, believing that the two telarians had perished.

The two youths who tried to hide were nowhere in sight.

CHAPTER FOUR

"NICOLE, WAKE UP!" yelled Alex through the bars of the cell to the other side of the room where his sister was lying still inside of another cell. "By the trinity, please wake..."

Alex's words were interrupted by Nicole moaning as she turned onto her side.

"Nicole!" he called.

Nicole sat up and started rubbing her left shoulder with her right hand.

"Ow my flippin' back," she said.

"Nicole, over here," called Alex.

Nicole got up and walked over to the bars and said, "I see they caught you. 'Suppose you're not as fast a runner as you claim."

"Cut me some slack sis, I'm only telarian. I still get winded and tired when I run. Besides, what use is being strong if you get caught?"

"I was doing quite fine...just...someone got me from behind."

"See if you can bend those bars open," he said.

Nicole grabbed a hold of the bars and tried to pull them apart, while the other prisoners watched on with hope, but to no avail. "Not even a budge," she said hopelessly.

Alex huffed as he threw his hands in his face with frustration.

"Lets' pray that we get some help before they take us wherever they plan to take us."

***

After shifting around between folded airspaces and shifting scenery, they landed in darkness.

Not a room, but a cavern.

The air was cold and old. The stone wall was wet. The echo of dripping water from somewhere deep below.

The air within was cool and unmoving, heavy with age and the faint mineral scent of stone which had never been familiar with sunlight.

Darkness dominated the space, not the absence of light, but a deliberate, consuming shadow, as if illumination itself had been unwelcomed here in the cavern for at least a century.

The only exception being the light created from within.

Sound, the regular kind, often behaved strangely, swallowed quickly, footsteps muted as though the mountain listened and chose not to echo.

The cavern widened as it descended, its walls rising high and uneven, formed of jagged black rock threaded with veins of dull crystal which occasionally caught and distorted what little light dared enter.

These veins of the sanctuary pulsed faintly, irregularly, like a slow, subterranean heartbeat.

The stone bore markings, etched, gouged, or burned into the surface, symbols too old to belong to any single language.

At the heart of the cavern's center, unseen but from above sat Convergence.

The ground there dipped inward, forming a vast circular depression, smooth as if melted rather than carved. The air above it shimmered subtly, bending perception. Distance felt unreliable and depth uncertain. Shadows stretched and recoiled without a clear source, as though responding to something unseen moving just beyond reality's skin.

A low vibration permeated the space, not loud enough to hear, but strong enough to be felt in the bones. It carried with it a sense of pressure, of time folding inward, of moments pressing against one another one after the other.

Standing near the Convergence often produced the unsettling impression that the past, present, and future were no longer neatly separated, but stacked, compressed, and waiting.

The ceiling above rose into darkness, disappearing entirely, though occasionally a faint glow would ripple across the stone as if distant lightning flashed behind it, echoes of the proverbial approaching storm outside bleeding through layers of rock and myth. Stalactites hung like broken teeth, some fractured, others deliberately shaped, hinting that the mountain itself had been altered to accommodate what lay within.

Nothing within the cavern felt accidental.

Mount Sinovian was not merely sheltering the Convergence. It was reinforcing her and is one of many entry points for the Convergence throughout the known and unknown galaxies.

And even in stillness, there was the unmistakable sense that the cavern was holding its breath, waiting for the moment when the Convergence would no longer be satisfied with silence.

As they moved to the center, Christina stumbled forward, catching herself.

Steve steadied her.

"Where are we?" Christina whispered, the words swallowed by the dark.

Steve's throat worked. "Mount Sinovian..."

Her head snapped towards him as she believed that she was hallucinating at first.

"Steve, this place is forbidden," she said.

Before he could continue, the multiplexed voice returned, calmer now, closer.

"Do not fear."

A faint light appeared, dim at first, then brightening into a clean beam which struck the cavern floor like a spotlight.

And in that light sat five medallions.

Golden.

Ancient.

Not jewelry, but keys.

Each bore a symbol etched into its face: encircled lightning, flamed fist, wolf, moon-star, and the leader's mark, a pyramid with an eye at the center.

Steve knelt automatically, as if his body recognized what his mind hadn't caught up to yet. He picked them up carefully and placed them in Christina's hands.

They were warm.

Alive.

Christina stared at them. "What are these?"

"Consider them awakeners," Convergence said. "They are not gifts. The gifts were planted at birth. These call your gifts fully to the surface."

Christina's pulse thudded. "I see two of them match tattoos on my and Steves' wrist. The others, where are they?"

"Taken."

"Hiding."

"Running."

Christina gripped the medallions tighter. "Then send us to them."

A pause, like the Trinity was weighing her.

"You will find them. The medallions in conjunction with the marks on your wrist will help you make the connections. And when the five stand together...you shall all return to me at once and Telari will learn to defend itself through you."

The darkness deepened for a heartbeat...and then, the cavern vanished.

***

Christina and Steve reappeared in a wooded area, dense trees, shadowed undergrowth, the smell of damp earth.

Christina spun briefly, searching for the darkness with the medallions clutched to her

28

chest, registering late, they were no longer in the cavern.

"Convergence, wait…"

A voice cut her off.

"Well, well," Shanna said, stepping from between trees with a smile like a knife. "Isn't this an unexpected surprise. I thought you were terminated, but no matter, we'll finish the job now."

Christina's stomach dropped.

Shanna raised her hand.

"Take them."

The shaytans opened fire.

Steve threw both hands up instinctively.

And something answered.

A yellow shield snapped into existence, smooth, shimmering, catching laser bolts like rain striking glass.

Christina stared at the barrier, shocked.

Steve stared at his own hands.

"I didn't," he began.

Christina's wrist burned again.

And her eyes, without her permission, glowed.

Shanna leapt, bow already in hand, drawing in midair.

Christina didn't speak.

She *thought* one word.

Sleep.

Shanna's body slackened in the air.

Her bow and arrow slipped free.

A falcon swept down and snatched the arrow as soon as it was released from the bow and then flew off as the bow fell to the ground.

Simultaneously Shanna crashed into the dirt with a sound which made even the shaytans hesitate to get to her.

From behind a nearby tree, Kevin watched, heart pounding as the falcon returned to him with the arrow.

"Thank you," he said quietly.

And for the first time in his life, the animals weren't just warning him.

They were hoping for a change with him.

CHAPTER FIVE

KEVIN LOOKED ON with a pleased expression of hope as the two strangers vanished.

"Where'd they go?" asked Shanna, waking up and pushing herself off the ground in anger.

Christina and Steve reappeared standing behind Kevin and out of site of the huntress and the shaytans.

Christina put a finger over her lips, signaling the stranger not to say a word.

Steve pointed a finger in the direction of the huntress, and the sky darkened.

From out of nowhere, five large gray wolves appeared to emerge from behind some of the trees and they started inching towards the huntress and her shaytans, all from different directions.

As the wolves started growling and drooling, Shanna looked around angrily for Christina and Steve while keeping an eye on the approaching wolves.

She then growled in anger.

"Wherever you are, I'll find you, and you'll belong to my lord," she said.

The evil huntress then pushed a button on her left wrist and a small ship appeared hovering over her and the small group of shaytans.

The shaytan empire's smaller aircrafts were compact, quiet, and utilitarian, designed for travel between villages, patrol duties, and short atmospheric flights as well as having a contrast light speed function to toss them across galaxies. These crafts were smooth-bodied and slightly asymmetrical, shaped more like living organisms than machines. Their hulls curved naturally, with no sharp edges, appearing grown rather than assembled.

The surface material had a muted metallic sheen, often tinted green, bronze, or charcoal, reflecting the sky rather than standing out against it. Propulsion was nearly silent, no roaring engines, producing only a low harmonic hum when close.

The windows were absent; instead, pilots rely on internal visual systems. Landing gears folded seamlessly into the hull, allowing the craft to settle gently into fields, forest clearings, or village outskirts without damaging the land as well as teleportation beams which could whisk troops away from the planets' surface at a moments' notice.

These ships were numerous and standardized, recognizable across Telari, symbolizing presence rather than power.

A beam of light projected down onto the huntress and her troops and pulled them up, before taking off.

The ship then disappeared into the sky.

The gray wolves soon vanished as if they had never been there.

Kevin then looked at the two strangers and noticed they had tattoos on their wrists which were almost similar to his own.

"Who are you?" he asked.

Christina extended her hand and said, "I am Christina and this is Steve," Steve smiled and Kevin reciprocated by taking her hand and smiling back at Steve as she continued. "We were sent by Convergence."

Kevin walked around her while looking at the ground.

"I am Kevin," he said.

He continued walking in a circle.

"Convergence wants us to fight back, right?" he asked.

"The Trinity has given each of us a gift which will help us to defend our home."

Kevin looked at the tattoo of the wolf on his wrist and shook his head in the negative. "All I can do is talk to animals, but I'm willing to help in any way I can!"

"Individually, it may seem like an insurmountable task, but I believe with five of us together, we should at least be able to put a dent in their forces," said Christina.

She then pulled a medallion out of her satchel with the symbol of a wolf on it, and it matched Kevin's tattoo exactly.

Kevin examined the medallion and then put it around his neck. The wolf lit up for a brief second and the medallion seemed to turn into a light as it recessed into his chest.

Without warning, Kevin's body started shifting and twisting as he changed into a large gray wolf.

"He can change into a wolf!" acknowledged Steven. "Cool!"

All of a sudden Kevin morphed from the wolf into a Harpy eagle.

Then a squirrel.

Then a bull.

Then a large black panther. He roared majestically.

"That can come in handy," agreed Christina.

Kevin then morphed back into himself and stared at his hands in disbelief.

"Now all we have to do is find the two whose names are Alex and Nicole," said Christina as her telepathic abilities continued growing.

"Who?" asked Kevin as the trio started walking off.

***

"You have summoned me my lord?" asked Gaylor as he stepped in front of a giant viewing screen with Desatyr, a hideous, demonic looking figure, on the giant screen, dominating it.

Desatyr stood at the apex of the shaytan empire.

Desatyr was three times the size of a standard shaytan, a towering colossus whose presence alone inspired paralysis. His frame was massive and imposing, armored in natural bone plating and other unatural enhancements which marked him as both ruler and executioner. His ears pointy and long.

Unlike many shaytans, Desatyr's greatest weapon is his combination of strength and intellect, features not earned in honesty.

Desatyr was calculating, articulate, and patient. Where others revel in immediate violence, Desatyr preferred delayed and extended torture and the opportunity to enjoy the suffering of his enemies.

Desatyr understood psychology, culture, and fear at a level which allowed him to dismantle whole civilizations without unnecessary expenditure of energy or resources.

His voice was layered, deep, resonant, and impossible to ignore, carrying authority which felt almost gravitational. When Desatyr spoke, silence followed, not because it was commanded, but because no one dared to interrupt.

Desatyr saw himself as destruction incarnate, the architect of death in this universe, as well as others.

The technology he had amassed over the decades has helped him to become the most feared ruler in the known universe to date.

To him, Telari was not a world, it was a weigh station, meant to become his pit stop for assessing, refueling, acquiring resources, and making his jump clean into an adjacent galaxy known only as the milky way.

Taking Telari was a must.

"I see you have managed to gather a sizeable multitude on our first return here and I congratulate you on a job well done."

"Thank you, my lord," replied Gaylor as he bowed. "This world is as simple as you stated."

"But the vispot orb has informed me that there are five Telarians who can potentially be problematic for me. They were born of Convergence. I believe you have captured two of them," he said with a deep monstrous voice.

"Yes, my lord, I believe they share familial ties," started Gaylor. "Shanna said there was a brown skinned woman and a beige colored man who vanished at one of the village domiciles. They were unsure if it was the disruptor cannons which took them or not, also I am uncertain as to why they are more special than the others."

"They live; I can sense it. But they must not be destroyed, I need them captured, alive, for...research!"

"Yes my lord," replied Gaylor as he bent over, bidding adieu to the demon

The large screen went black.

Gaylor then vanished in a puff of red smoke.

CHAPTER SIX

ALEX PACED BACK and forth in anxiousness, as Nicole just stood from her cell and watched him.

The cavern in which they were kept, didn't smell stale, but the accumulating body odor of all who was captured didn't make the environment smell welcomed either.

If one had to go to the bathroom, you cold alert a shaytan soldier and they might take you to a bathroom. If you were returned to a cell, you were lucky.

Anyone who wasn't returned to a cell, was assumed to have been consumed almost immediately by the monstrous looking shaytans.

Most of the captured telarians opted to try to hold their bodily functions in until they could no longer do so, or go into the corners of the cells, abandoning all cares of modesty.

"Will you stop doing that?" she asked of her brothers' pacing.

"I'm sorry, but I can't help it," replied Alex. "I pace when I'm nervous."

"As you should be," interjected Gaylor who seemed to have come from nowhere. "I've just been informed that the two of you must live, which means there is probably a fate far worse than death for you both."

Suddenly, a bird, resembling a falcon, flew into a nearby window as Gaylor looked at with curiosity.

The falcon then flew towards the space popper and morphed into a giant lion as it landed on him, causing him to scream with anger.

"YOU STUPID BEAST, I'LL HAVE YOU FOR SUPPER TONIGHT!"

The lion roared loudly while starting to drool on the fallen space popper.

Gaylor then developed a look of fear on his face and then suddenly vanished in a puff of red smoke.

The lion then quickly morphed into a large wolf which then howled as Alex, Nicole, as well as the other captured telarians watched nervously.

A second later, Christina and Steve appeared standing in front of the two cells.

The wolf then morphed into Kevin as Nicole and Alex watched in astonishment.

Christina looked at the two medallions in her satchel as she pulled them out. She then passed the one with the lightning bolt on its face to Alex and the one with the flaming fist to Nicole.

They both put the medallions on and just like with Kevin, they lit up and retreated inside of their chests.

Armed shaytan soldiers soon darted into the room.

Alex, Nicole, Steven, Kevin, Christina and the captured telarians all vanished from out of the cells.

***

The cavern breathed its fresh air onto their young faces.

The stone walls stretched upward into darkness, damp and ancient, as if Mount Sinovian itself were alive and listening. The faint echo of dripping water marked time in slow, patient beats.

The five young adults had mystically appeared in the darkened cavern as various areas within it started to light up faintly.

Christina stood at the center, Steve beside her, the satchel now empty at her waist.

Five medallions no longer inside, all standing huddled together.

"The rest of our people?" queried Nicole.

"Safe in Humania," replied Steve as Christina smiled.

No longer waiting to join their teammates, Christina looked up to the dark void as her eyes started to glow a bright yellow.

A low vibration rolled through the ground, felt more than heard, and the multiplexed voice returned, calmly.

"As you know," started Convergence, "the enemy gathers your people. To enslave them. To consume them."

Nicole's voice cut through the dark, sharp with anger. "Then stop talking and tell us what to do!"

"You're of value to us young one, but your tone with us will not always be tolerated...we suggest you watch it!"

Nicole looked down and then back up. "My apologies."

"The anger and frustration you all have is understood and appreciated but now is not the time to be irrational and rageful, for I have armed you to defend this world as you see fit!"

A faint glow rippled across the cavern floor.

"You already know how this was done but allow me to expand on your knowledge."

A light shone down on Alex. The lit image of his medallion flipped forward out of his chest, growing with each flip.

Lightning etched in gold.

The image then flipped backward, still growing with each flip until it was large enough to completely flip over him. The rim flared as it vanished.

The lightning symbol burst into blue-white light and sank into him like liquid fire.

Alex gasped.

The cavern *answered*.

A beam of electric blue energy dropped from above, wrapping him in spiraling bands of light. The air cracked as if charged.

Alex cried out, not in pain, but shock, as the light reshaped him.

Black fabric flowed over his body like shadow racing ahead of him, forming a tight, aerodynamic suit which clung cleanly at every joint. Blue armored pads locked into place at his knees and elbows. His boots formed next, sleek, flexible, built for impact and then his gloves, fingers twitching with barely restrained energy.

A blue eye-mask sealed over his face. A fitted cap settled low.

His eyes ignited, blue-white lightning flickering behind them.

The beam vanished.

Alex staggered, then steadied himself.

"I..." He looked down at his hands. "I feel like I could outrun sound."

"And light itself," Convergence said. "You are Altimari the speed of your collective."

Alex laughed once, breathless. "Whoa."

A light then dropped down over Nicole.

"Hit me," she said smilingly.

Fire exploded outward but didn't burn as the lit image of her medallion flipped forward, growing with each flip.

The fist on fire.

The image then flipped backward, still growing with each flip until it flipped over her.

The rim flared as it vanished, just as it had done with her twin.

A red-gold beam engulfed Nicole, heat rippling the air. The black combat weave sealed around her torso first, locking in place like reinforced muscle. Red boots slammed into form, heavy and solid. Red bracers climbed her forearms in segmented plates. A red mask framed her eyes as a gold rimmed red belt snapped into place at her waist.

Her red hair spilled free, flowing down her back like a banner.

Nicole clenched her fists.

The stone beneath her feet cracked.

Her eyes glowed, embers trapped behind glass.

She grinned. "Oh... I *like* this!"

"You are Nirvana," Convergence intoned. "The unbreakable strength of your collective."

Nicole rolled her shoulders, testing her weight. "Yeah. I can work with this."

A light then shone down on Kevin as he looked up smilingly. The lit image of his medallion flipped forward, growing with each flip.

The eyes of the wolf image glowed.

The image then flipped backward, still growing with each flip until it flipped over him. The rim flared as it vanished.

Kevin took a breath.

A dark beam fell, so deep it almost swallowed illumination itself.

Black fur-textured material wrapped Kevin's body, smooth and living, forming a bodysuit which absorbed light instead of reflecting it. A purple leather mantle dropped over his shoulders, fastened at the collar, the massive paw symbol embossed centered on his belt.

Purple boots and gloves locked into place; claws hinted at the belt buckle and on their ridges.

Kevin's eyes flashed, gold, green, shadow, cycling through animal instincts behind his purple mask until they finally stopped at a purple hue.

His body shuddered.

For half a second, his outline *shifted quickly,* wolf, shark, eagle, panther, before snapping back into human form.

Kevin exhaled, wide-eyed. "I... I can feel them... All of them."

"You are Kalgorie," said Convergence. "Guardian of the wild part of your collective, with focus, you can shift your form into any animal."

The light then fell upon Steve as he swallowed hard.

The lit image of his medallion flipped forward, growing with each flip.

The crescent moon within the star.

The image then flipped backward, still growing with each flip until it flipped over him. The rim flared and then vanished.

Steve's hands trembled. "Chris..."

"You've already been doing this your whole life with a book," she said softly. "Now, you are the book!"

Green light surged, wrapping him in clean, angular planes, the moon, and stars danced into his body. Black armor plates locked into place over a fitted base. Green gloves, boots, belt, each forming with deliberate precision. A deep green cape unfurled behind him, heavy at the shoulders, etched faintly with runic patterns.

A green mask sealed over his eyes.

They glowed, soft, refracted green, like light through glass and like the skies of Telari itself.

The air around his hands shimmered, reality thinning.

Steve let out a shaky laugh. "This... is good."

"You are Shryer," Convergence said. "Architect of illusion as part of your collective."

Only one remained.

Christina smiled at Shryer and stared upward.

The light which fell upon her was absolute.

A column of golden radiance descended upon her and elevated her, without her medallion emerging for she was primed as central, quiet and commanding. Her armor formed in articulated plates, golden, radiant, fitted perfectly to her body.

Black underlayers framed her arms and legs, emphasizing strength and speed. Gold gloves, boots, and mask sealed into place.

Her dark hair flowed freely.

Her eyes glowed, warm amber, steady and unblinking under her golden mask.

The cavern seemed to lean in towards her.

When the light faded, Christina stood taller, not physically, but in presence and ahead of the other four with her.

"You are Cherokee," Convergence declared. "The head of this collective. Leader of the Guards of Telari. These are now your identities, who you were, will now be your disguises!"

Cherokee looked at the others.

Altimari. Nirvana. Kalgorie. Shryer.

Her team.

She placed her hand over her chest.

"We won't fail you Convergence."

The others followed, hands to their chests.

Together, they spoke, not rehearsed, not commanded.

It felt remembered.

"For the Trinity. For Telari!"

The cavern trembled, not in fear, but in recognition.

CHAPTER SEVEN

THE STREETS OF Gadascar were filled with people running and screaming as they tried to elude capture from the shaytan warriors

Physically, shaytans bear an unsettling resemblance to what Earth cultures have long imagined as demons, an irony they take pride in.

They are average sized, grotesque humanoids, with elongated limbs and hunched postures that suggest both intelligence and animal readiness.

Their skin tones range from dark obsidian to sickly crimson and ashen gray, often textured or ridged rather than smooth. Pointed ears, sharply angled and expressive, rise from their skulls like blades.

Their faces were deeply unsettling: sunken or glowing eyes adapted to low-light environments, wide, predatory mouths lined with serrated teeth, deeply angry facial expressions which seemed permanently fixed between hunger and contempt.

Shaytans are carnivorous, with a particular craving for intelligent species. Consumption is not just biological, it is symbolic. To eat another sentient being is to assert superiority, to absorb dominance. Derivative humanoid type flesh, in particular, is prized for its emotional resonance and resistance, making conquest all the more satisfying.

They do not see this merely as cruelty, to them, it is natural order.

It was well known by all of the inhabitants of the planet Telari that if you were ever captured, you were made a slave or a meal. Sometimes you were both.

"There's no trace of them anywhere around here sir," said one of the shaytans who was on a horse looking at the various people scurry out of the way.

"Keep looking and gather up as many of these pathetic Telarians as you can, they're around here somewhere," said Gaylor as the hover craft he was on descended next to the horse.

The horse, carrying the shaytan, galloped off as the space popping general signaled the other troops to gather up as many Telarians as they could. One of the shaytans grabbed a hooded woman and shoved her into the back of a hover cage with other Telarians.

As the door to the back of the hover cage closed, the woman brushed her hood back slightly, revealing Nicole in her ordinary garb. She smiled briefly.

***

After watching the woman get placed in the hover craft, a large Harpy eagle, flew high in the sky above from Gadascar to the dark forest of

Tenacia, where Christina, Steve and Alex were waiting

They watched as the eagle descended and morphed into Kevin in his Telarian form as he touched the ground.

"They just put her into the vehicle," started Kevin. "I also saw the space popper and the huntress there."

"Those two are gonna be a problem," replied Steve as Alex nodded his head in agreement.

Christina looked down at the symbol tattooed on her wrist and said, "Not as much of a problem as we're going to be to them."

***

As the prisoners of the shaytans slowly followed each other into the six cells, which were positioned three on three across from each other, a shaytan noticed the hooded figure looking around.

"You!" he shouted as he pointed to Nicole.

She turned and looked at the shaytan.

"Remove that hood," he said angrily.

Nicole removed the hood from off of her head and the shaytan signaled her to keep moving.

Nicole kept walking, following the slow single file line into the cell which was soon closed as the last person was shoved in by one of the shaytans.

All six cells were full to the point where the telarians inside had very little room to move around.

Nicole sighed in frustration.

Young telarian children were crying in various cells.

This angered Nicole.

Gaylor soon walked into the dreary room. "My telarian friends," He started, " some of you will get the distinct pleasure of serving my lordship, day in and day out until you die at which time you will serve him one last time by giving him nourishment. Some of you will be able to feed him almost immediately and your sacrifices in his honor will be greatly appreciated."

Gaylor paced back and forth in front of the cells and smiled.

Nicole looked at the space popper curiously. *He doesn't look like the rest of them,* she thought. *What's his motive for doing this?*

Gaylor then signaled four shaytans to position themselves in front of the six cells in a two-by-two formation.

After the shaytans complied, he popped out of sight leaving a puff of red smoke.

As the crowds in opposing cells started to chatter, Nicole sighed out in relief that the space popper had not recognized her.

A harpy eagle flew high above toward the makeshift lair created by the shaytans and he landed on a perch just left to a window.

The lair was formerly a government tribunal building, the telarian leaders gathered there were among the first attacked during this latest wave of Shaytan Empire attacks.

The building was multilayered with the ground level being the level where the prisoners were kept. The layer above was currently unoccupied, and the level below is where Gaylor kept in communique with the emperor through video feeds.

Unseen by the shaytans, the eagle quickly morphed into a mouse while landing into the windowsill and squeaked loudly, several times.

The eyes of the mouse met Nicole's, and she acknowledged his presence with a nod and a smile.

The mouse then scurried into a nearby hole.

The mouse ran through the maze-like crevices looking as if he were searching for a piece of cheese. The mouse came across two other mice, and he squeaked to them several times.

One of the mice squeaked back and gestured behind where he had just come from.

Then Kalgorie, the mouse, moved further through a narrow passageway and then turned left. As he emerged from a hole, he spotted a glowing red sphere on a large monitor.

The sphere was significant and Kalgorie knew it, though he wasn't sure how or why he knew it. As he continued to look at the monitor, he could tell the area where the emperor spoke from was of high importance.

Standing in front of the monitor was the space popper.

"...did not see any of the specials my lord," said Gaylor nervously.

"You and Shanna are both fools," started the hideous Shaytan Emperor. "Find those Telarians and bring them to me at once!"

"My Lord Desatyr," started a voice from off screen where the emperor was located. "We're ready to transport the telarians up here."

"Stand-by for Gaylor's command," replied the emperor.

"Yes, my lord."

The mouse then ran back almost the same way he had come and emerged out of a hole which was outside of the middle cell door.

The mouse suddenly morphed into a large silverback gorilla, shocking the shaytans as well as the prisoners in the cage.

The gorilla beat his chest as he roared and then immediately grabbed the heads of two of the shaytans and clunked them together. He then ducked down instinctively as one of the shaytans swung at his head, missing the gorilla. The gorilla then gave him a wild upper cut, causing the shaytan to fly up and hit the ceiling. Hard. Before hitting the floor. Even Harder.

Nicole put her hand over her chest, and the lit medallion flew forward, flipping through the people in the tight quarters as it grew in size.

It then flipped backward and over Nicole, changing her into Nirvana.

Nirvana quickly moved to the bars of the cell and spread them apart as if they were clay.

She moved quickly to the other cells as telarians climbed out excitedly and did the same thing, freeing all the prisoners.

The gorilla then morphed into a gray rhino as Nirvana jumped on his back and as he charged into the south wall, knocking it down as they ran through.

The freed prisoners cheered as they started following the two out.

Suddenly a multitude of shaytans showed up out of nowhere and started to accost the people with their weapons when without warning, a blue blur moved through the shaytans and disarmed them, causing them a look of confusion.

Cherokee descended from high above and telepathically lifted the shaytans, transporting them into the cells where the Telarians were being held.

Shryer then magically walked in there out of thin air and resealed the bars to the cells with magic. He then floated backwards out of the lair while waving to the shaytans as they all just looked at each other.

The damaged wall then repaired itself magically.

A fraction of a second later, a red puff of smoke introduced Gaylor as he looked around at the cells with anger.

He roared loudly!

CHAPTER EIGHT

AS CHRISTINA LOOKED from the wooded area to the small town of Humania, she saw an image of the huntress, Shanna, instructing shaytans to gather up some of the towns inhabitants.

"It is as I expected," started Christina. "As soon as we freed the captives, they double their efforts and try to take more."

"So how 'bout we go on the offensive," started Alex, "Take down their deployment ships and then their mothership!"

"That is a good plan," agreed Steve,

Christina nodded her head. "It can work, but we need to do this right. Kevin what did you learn?"

Kevin held out his hand and a small orb raised up off his hand.

The orb started displaying three-dimensional images of the temporary layer with a viewscreen in a room where Gaylor was speaking with the shaytan emperor.

"They have three generals," started Kevin, "what I've noticed about their generals is, that there is always some sort of red smoke briefly around them. The space popper, the huntress, and the one they call Kishi. When I saw the image of the shaytan emperor on the viewer, there was the red vispot orb emanating the same red smoke."

"We take out that vispot orb on the mother ship..."started Steve.

"Then we take away their abilities," finished Kevin.

Christina's eyes started glowing. "I don't think taking out the orb is going to take away their abilities, but worse than that, I think it does more than give them their abilities, I think it's also controlling them."

"What does it matter?" asked Nicole. "Their slaughtering our people, and those who are still alive are being enslaved."

"We have to try and free those generals too," started Christina "Sometimes we have to do what we don't like in order to meet the path of less resistance. The generals are the brains outside of the shaytan emperor, We get rid of the generals..."

"Their troops will be clueless idiots without orders," added Nicole.

"So what's the call?" asked Steve.

Christina smiled. "Sometimes I find a direct approach is best!"

Kevin put the holographer away as they all stood up and looked in the direction of Humania.

"For the Trinity. For Telari," they all proclaimed and they then placed their hand on their chest,

From five Telarians, a gold discs of light emanated from each and started flipping bigger, growing in size. The lights then started flipping back as it grew until it passed over each of the Telarians, transforming them in their battle armor.

Cherokee, Shryer, Kalgorie, Nirvana and Altimari stood there, each in full costume."

Kalgorie morphed into a large black panther and roared. He then took off toward Humania.

Altimari then ran off in a blue blur.

Shryer encased Nirvana in a yellow bubble and took off, flying to Humania with Nirvana in tow.

Cherokee lifted off in flight.

***

Shanna saw them first and growled.

The black panther ran straight for her as she aimed her bow and arrow at the large cat.

Try not to take her life, said Cherokee from inside his head.

Kalgorie roared and then leapt.

Shanna fired.

The black panther morphed into a snake and the arrow flew closely by him but missed him as he quickly reached Shanna and wrapped himself around the huntress and pulled her down.

Kalgorie then started to squeeze as Shanna resisted while grunting.

Shanna soon passed out as Kalgorie the snaked unwound from the huntress and then morphed into a lion.

He roared loudly as the shaytans started to surround him and then ran off.

Shryer immediately turned the ropes securing the prisoners into loose vines as they cheered and ran off into multiple directions. He then produced chains which wrapped around Shanna with locks all up and down the length of her body which clicked lock.

***

Five shaytans ran straight for Nirvana.

The first one she quickly gave him an uppercut and then grabbed the back of his head before he could get too far. She then slammed his head into the ground.

Then two more shaytans approached, and she quickly grabbed an arm from each, spun them around and threw them a hundred and twenty yards away.

The last two growled at her angrily and she roared back at them.

They turned to run and she forward kicked one in the back, slamming him into a large tree.

The fifth one turned around and started shaking

"BOO!" she yelled and he fell backwards.

***

Altimari zipped through the long line of captives and knocked out the shaytans one by one, unknown that he was being watched by Gaylor the space popper.

As Altimari reached the last shayman, he went to strike him and in a flash of red smoke, Gaylor popped in and caught his hand, stopping

him too fast, Altimari screamed as he felt
something in his right arm shatter.

POOF.

A punch in the face.

POOF.

An elbow in the back.

POOF.

A leg sweep knocking Altimari down.

Cherokee felt and saw him simultaneously
as her eyes started glowing blue.

Gaylor popped out one more time but this
time something was different.

Altimari could see his form disappearing in
one area and starting to reappear in another
area right after the appearance of the red
smoke.

He was watching Gaylor as he was changing
locations.

Altimari rolled to the left and was able to
catch Gaylor in just enough time to cup the back
of his head with his left hand and slam it into
the shaytans' head, rendering them both
unconscious as he finally fell to the ground,
right arm in severe pain.

Cherokee's eyes turned yellow as she looked
around.

Shryer was creating mirrors around some of
the shaytans causing them to look confused as
they ran out of one mirror and into another
mirror.

Shryer, please tend to Altimari's injuries,
said Cherokee's voice from inside his head.

Shryer walked into an invisible doorway and then reappeared next to Altimari who was starting to stand.

"Whoa there fellow guard," he started, "let me have a look!" He waved a hand over Altimari and could see his skeletal structure, the only injury observed was a right arm triple fracture. "Corpus tuum sanitaria!"

Shryer then watched as Altimaris' arm healed itself.

Altimari rotated his right arm, "Gee thanks!"

Shryer smiled. "No 'I' in Guards!"

***

The large lion grabbed a shaytan and threw him into a tree!

Another shaytan jumped up and came down over the lion with a sharp sword and was about to pierce Kalgorie.

The lion quickly morphed down into a mouse as the sword slammed down into the ground.

The mouse quickly morphed into a gorilla and slammed down with two fists over the shaytan.

The shaytan fell silent as the gorilla beat his chest looking around at all the felled shaytans.

"Have we freed them all?" asked Nirvan.

"Yes we have!" proclaimed Cherokee as they all cheered with excitement just as a large ship showed up over head, causing them to look up.

Beams of light fell on the fallen huntress and Gaylor, and they vanished into the ship.

"SHRYER...BRING IT DOWN!"

Shryer started to wave his hands as the little demon Kishi soon landed in the midst of the group.

"Atah, atah, atah, KISHI!" yelled Kishi just as Cherokees eyes widened with realization of what his ability was.

"SHRYER! THROW A FORCEFIELD AROUND HIM!"

The order came too late.

Kishi's body stated shivering real fast and then -

KABOOM!

When the smoke cleared, The Guards of Telari were sprawled out on the ground, all unconscious but Nirvana and Cherokee.

Nirvana passed out as soon as her eyes met Cherokees'.

Cherokee could hear her own heartbeat as her eyes started to blur, and as the warship was speeding off.

Then there was darkness.

CHAPTER NINE

GAYLOR AND SHANNA waited in the darkness of the Throne room on their knees with their heads bowed down as Desatyr, the shaytan emperor, bestowed his hideous presence upon them.

His movements sounded wet, even though he was a biped, walking slowly around the two.

"I miscalculated the intelligence of the orb," he started. "That is a mistake I won't make again. The Convergence is truly more powerful than I had previously believed, but no matter, their efforts to create guardians for this pathetic, technologically devoid planet, will prove fruitless when I destroy them all!"

"My lord," started Gaylor, they are powerful, though they are few, they seemed to be well coordinated and..."

"SILENCE!" yelled Desatyr as Shanna looked at Gaylor and shook her head in the negative, suggesting he not say another word.

Desatyr continued, "I spared your lives and had the vispot orb imbue you with gifts for my soul purpose of tracking the human descendants across the galaxies to satisfy my hunger and the annoying presence of these

Telarian guards, is but a minor setback in my ultimate conquest."

The shaytan emperor took a breath. "I guess I cannot blame you, after all there were only three of you and there are five of them!"

He walked around Shanna and Gaylor, and drew a nefarious grin on his face.

"I am going to supply assistance in dealing with these so-called Guards."

Three large holographic screens appeared high above them. "My shaytans are incapable of receiving power from the orb, but I do have more prisoners who I think will suffice!"

The screens scrolled through several of Desatyr's prisoners, those kept alive after combat because he saw something in each of them, he felt he would be able to exploit one day.

The three screens soon stop on three suitable candidates.

"Vael," started the emperor," once an archivist and a keeper of records of history on his planet, I captured him for knowing too much. The vispot orb will give him the ability to generate zones of null interference. My enemies powers will weaken, any transformations will destabilize, and confusion will ensue. Though he is not able to take away powers, to the guards it will feel like he has. He will be taking away, intention."

On the screen you can see the red smoke take hold around Vael as his eyes become deep voids, and he then he vanishes in a puff of red smoke.

"Next is Sereth," continued Desatyr, "she was a mother, and a warrior who surrendered herself willingly to me in order to save her family, to save her children. Little does she know, I still consumed her entire family. In addition to my control, her will to fight for her family who she thinks is still alive will make her extremely loyal. The vispot orb will influence her protective instinct into uncontainable combustion, her emotional spikes will be an explosive force, her fear will create shockwaves, her love a burning aura, all difficult for her to control except when she can project those emotions to whomever she wants...weakening an opponent."

The red smoke encircled her and started creating small red fissures all over her body. She then vanished from out of her cell.

"And lastly, there is Threx the Untamed. He is actually closer aligned with my design than the rest of you. On his planet, he was a thief and survivalist, clever, selfish, adaptable. The vispot orb will cause his body to refuse stability. He will be able to partially phase, stretch, harden, or dissolve instinctively. He will adapt to any fight unpredictably."

The red smoke took a hold of him and he soon vanished.

Three red beams of light appeared in between Gaylor and and Shanna and the three warriors appeared in the three respective spots.

Vael stood taller than the others, his frame unnaturally thin, his limbs long and angular, as if gravity had never fully claimed him. His skin was a dull, bruised purple, stretched tight over sharp bone, and his head was elongated, Martian in shape, with no visible hair or ornamentation.

Where eyes should have been there were deep, lightless voids, not black, but *empty*, swallowing reflection and depth alike. The red smoke around him did not curl or drift; it hung motionless, as if afraid to move, but then soon vanished.

The air near him felt wrong. Sound softened. Thought slowed. Standing too close to Vael felt like standing inside hesitation itself.

Sereth stood with her shoulders squared, posture still that of a protector, even as the red smoke coiled tightly around her like a living shroud before it vanished. Her body was powerful, honed by combat, her beige-toned skin marred by glowing fissures which pulsed faintly beneath the surface, like magma trapped under stone.

Her face was almost human, almost. Where her nose was there were also three narrow slits on each side, opening and closing subtly as she breathed. Heat shimmered around her with every exhale.

Her eyes burned, not with rage, but with purpose. The kind that refused to die, no matter how much of the world has already been taken.

And then there was Threx, a half-man / half reptilian looking creature somewhere between the cross breed of an iguana and an alligator. Threx did not stand still, He couldn't. He rocked from side to side.

His body flickered at the edges, half-formed and unstable, a grotesque fusion of humanoid and reptilian anatomy. Scales rippled across his skin in uneven patterns, fading into flesh and then back again. His jaw was elongated, his teeth too many, his eyes sharp and restless, constantly adjusting.

Even as he breathed, his bones shifted beneath his skin, joints subtly reconfiguring, muscles tightening and loosening without conscious command. The red smoke around him crackled and warped, unable to decide what shape it should take, much like Threx himself, until it dissipated.

He smiled, and it was impossible to tell whether it was confidence...or hunger.

"Gaylor, do not disappoint me with this command," warned Desatyr.

"Yes my lord," answered Gaylor.

CHAPTER TEN

CHRISTINA, ALEX, KEVIN and Nicole all sat around a small table at the domicile unit once inhabited by Christina and Steve.

The domicile unit had once been modest but bright, the kind of place built for laughter rather than strategy. Christina had insisted on curtains that let the light in but softened it, and Steve had mounted shelves with careful precision, lining them with books, framed hand-crafted pictures, and small souvenirs from better days.

Now the windows were shattered.

Sheets of woven vine had been secured over the frames, snapping faintly whenever the wind pressed against them. The air inside still carried a faint trace of dust and something metallic— the lingering scent of explosives which had ripped through the village weeks earlier.

The front wall bore a jagged crack that ran from ceiling to floor, splitting the stone structure like a fault line. One corner of the living room ceiling gone, also covered by intertwined vines. The couch remained, though torn along one arm, stuffing exposed like pale bone beneath wounded fabric.

The Guards had moved in carefully at first, boots tracking soot across hardwood floors once polished by Christina every weekend. They had pushed the dining table against a reinforced interior wall and turned it into a command surface. Maps were spread where dinner plates had once rested. Another table, smaller, now used to eat off of.

Empty ration packs gathered in the kitchen sink.

Christina and Steve still smiled from behind cracked glass frames, forever unaware that their home had become a temporary stronghold.

At night, the Guards took turns resting in shifts.

The unit no longer felt like a home.

It felt like something holding its breath.

Steve soon joined them with some food he was able to scrounge up as he sat it on the table.

There looked to be there was barely enough food for three of them let alone five.

Steve then waved his hand up and then suddenly down as the food changed into a literal smorgasbord.

Alex started eating immediately as the others just looked at him.

"His running makes him hungry," Nicole said as everyone else started to eat, except for Kevin.

"What's wrong?" asked Steven as he pointed to the food. "Are you not hungry?"

"I am starving," replied Kevin. "I just don't eat items that come from animals."

A large salad bowl with vegetables appeared in front of him as well as another bowl filled with fruit slightly behind that one."

Kevin looked up at Steven and smiled.

"Have at it," said Steven.

Kevin then started eating.

Christina swirled her eating utensil around in her plate, not really picking up anything and appearing to have the weight of the world on her shoulders.

Steven noticed immediately.

"Chris?"

"We've messed up!" she started angrily as she dropped her fork in her plate. "We went in hot, weapons blazing and we shot off a warning shot!"

"We saved a lot of telarians today," started Alex as he paused from eating.

Nicole nodded. "They knocked us out and retrieved their remaining generals, but I definitely call this a win."

Kevin and Alex nodded in agreement as Steve looked at Christina.

He knew she knew much more.

"We showed them who we are too early in the game, I just wish I would've thought this through a little better...got people out quietly, not made so much noise..."

"We showed them exactly what we're capable of," argued Nicole.

"Exactly," started Christina, "we showed them exactly what we are, what we can do and gave them ideas of how we work," she paused. "And now," they're gonna use that knowledge to try and take us down."

"What, can you like...see the future or something?" asked Kevin.

"I can see variables, possibilities, but nothing absolute."

Everyone got quiet.

"Okay Cherokee," started Nicole, "I hear you! You tell us what you want us to do, and I will follow your lead,"

"We all will," added Kevin as he and the others nodded in the affirmative.

Christina managed a small smile as she lifted her fork to her mouth and started chewing, regaining confidence and feeling supported by her team. "The first thing I want you all to do, is eat up, we're gonna need the strength."

CHAPTER ELEVEN

THE VILLAGE OF Lathen Row was too quiet.

A scream heard by both Cherokee and Kalgorie had brought them there. They were ready to defend but the village seemed, empty.

Not abandoned, just muted. Doors were open. Fires burned low. Telarians were present and moved with purpose but avoided eye contact, their conversations hushed everything seeming unreal.

Kalgorie felt it first.

"The animals are gone?" he questioned quietly. "All of them," he then confirmed.

Cherokee stopped walking.

Altimari skidded to a halt beside her, boots scraping stone. "Gone how?"

"Fled," Kalgorie replied. His lights in his eyes shifted shades and traced the rooftops, the alleys, the tree line beyond the village wall, and the most subtle little print was seen.
"Something spooked them, and everything that could run did."

Shryer frowned, lifting a hand as yellow light shimmered faintly around his fingers, then flickered.

"...That's not good," he said as he shook his finger, an attempt to study the light.

The air shifted.

Not wind. Not pressure.

Absence.

Altimari took a step forward and nearly fell. "Whoa, okay, that's new," he said almost dismissively.

Cherokee felt it too. The thread she normally sensed between herself and the team, the quiet certainty, the *alignment,* dulled, as if wrapped in thick cloth.

"Everyone," she said evenly, "stay close."

A figure stood in the center of the square.

No flash. No sound.

Just there.

Tall. Lanky. Purple skin stretched thin over sharp bone. His frame looked unfinished, like something assembled without concern for comfort or balance.

He waited.

Vael's eyes were not eyes at all. They were voids, depthless, swallowing light, swallowing focus.

Shryer swallowed. "I don't like this."

Vael tilted his head.

The sound of the village dulled further. Footsteps softened. Breathing felt... optional.

Altimari clenched his fists. "Okay, big guy, if you're here to..."

He stopped.

Not because he couldn't speak.

Because he couldn't decide *how* to proceed.

Cherokee felt the hesitation ripple through them like a disease.

"No first attacks," she ordered sharply. "Defensive only!" She then tried to get a read on Vael but couldn't.

Vael raised one long, skeletal hand, not in attack, but acknowledgment.

Then he was gone.

The pressure lifted abruptly. Sound rushed back in, too loud, too sudden.

Altimari staggered, catching himself on a wall. "What the..."

"That was a probe," Shryer said, voice tight. "He didn't test our strength."

Kalgorie growled softly. "He's testing something."

Cherokee exhaled slowly.

"They know how we work," she said. "And they're about to push us."

As if summoned by her words, the ground shuddered.

A woman stepped from between two domiciles, her presence announced not by force, but by heat.

Cherokee doubled over in pain!

Mommy...mommy! The voices of the women's children from the beyond had reached Cherokee, unknown to Sereth.

The air warped around Sereth. Cracks of glowing red-gold light traced across her skin, pulsing faintly beneath the surface. Her shoulders were squared, posture disciplined, but her hands trembled.

She was crying.

Not sobbing.

Tears slid silently down her face, evaporating before they reached her jaw.

Nirvana took an involuntary step forward.

"Oh no," she whispered. "Somethings not right about this."

"You have no idea," agreed Cherokee.

Sereth looked over at Cherokee and then back at Nirvana.

Their eyes met.

The pressure wave hit.

Windows started shattering outward. Stone cracked beneath Nirvana's boots as she dropped into a defensive stance, muscles screaming as she absorbed the impact.

"Civilians!" Cherokee shouted.

Too late.

A blur moved along the edge of the square, something wrong, shifting.

Threx.

He didn't rush them. He *circled*, body flickering at the edges, limbs subtly reshaping with every step, learning.

Kalgorie, without shifting, produced the roar of the black panther.

Shanna's laughter echoed from a rooftop as Gaylor, in a puff of red smoke, popped in standing beside her.

"You should've stayed hidden," Shanna called. "This is where the lesson starts."

Cherokee raised her voice, steady despite the chaos.

"Defensive formation. Protect the villagers. Learn about your opposition swiftly."

High above, an unseen viewer drone was in the air, so Desatyr could watch.

In a puff of red smoke, Gaylor popped out from off the rooftop first.

Altimari bolted, looking for signs of the red smoke to appear so he could catch Gaylor first, then he started to slow.

"What in the..."

An uppercut from nowhere, sent him flying back twenty yards where he hit a wall and fell over.

"Why didn't I see that?" started Cherokee as she started to double over with a headache as Vael was making his way towards her from behind.

"Oh no you don't," said Shryer as he split himself in two, one to face Shanna and the other to help Cherokee.

Shanna quickly fired two arrows one hitting the Shryer approaching her in the left leg, the other Shryer getting hit in the right leg, a fraction of a second later.

He screamed as he snapped back into one Shryer with an arrow in each leg. He quickly fell to the ground.

Nirvana jumped high and prepared to come down hard on Shanna when she suddenly saw an image of her own mother and panicked.

Shanna back handed her and sent her flying to the ground where she crashed into creating a shallow crater.

Kalgorie morphed into a large wolf and headed straight towards Threx and as he got closer the back half of his body morphed into a snake while his front legs turned into wings, confusing him as he fell to the ground.

Threx raced towards Kalgorie while on all fours and bit hard on his right wing, causing the lion face to roar loudly in pain.

Cherokee looked to her far right and saw Altimari lying still and not moving.

She then looked to the left and saw Kalgorie on the ground, being mauled by Threx.

Shryer also on the ground with the arrows in his legs as the shaytans emerged in order to take him.

Nirvana lying on the ground in an uncompromising position, also not moving.

Cherokee then screamed as she stood fully up.

Vael was standing before her with his arm raised creating a low echoing scream reverberating over and over again in her head, attempting to confound her.

She forced a connection with the other guards.

"SHRYER GET US OUT OF HERE!"

Everything went black.

Then -

They were gone.

Desatyr himself descended to the surface via the yellow beam from the ship.

"Interesting," he said.

***

All she saw was blackness and then.

"Illuminaris!" proclaimed Shryer as the cavern in Mount Sinovian lit up.

The other four Guards were standing around her, looking fine as if nothing happened.

Cherokee breathed hard as she stood up. "You're all okay? I was right!"

"What happened to you back there?" asked Altimari.

"I...I don't know," started Cherokee, "The purple guy...reality altered...my mind shifted...instead of calculating probabilities...I lived one."

"What do you mean lived one?" asked Nirvana.

Shryer touched Cherokees' shoulder.

"Theres' more of them, there were five of them," stammered Cherokee. "I almost got you killed, I almost got you all killed...and that shaytan emperor..."

She took a breath. "He's definitely using the vispot orb to control his prisoners and imbuing them with powers."

The emotions overwhelmed her; she started gasping a little as Shryer steadied her.

"There's a woman they have with them," she started, "I believe she was trying to impose emotions on me but somehow a psychic link threw me through her to their emperor. She left her world willingly in order to serve him so he would spare her world and her children. She doesn't know it yet, but he destroyed all of them!"

"How do you know all this?" asked Nirvana.

"It is her job to know," said the tribunal voice of Convergence.

"This is too much for her!" yelled Nirvana, "Look at her!"

"And yet she saved you all from certain death, even when they had someone who could dampen your powers."

Cherokee stood up and her face started to look determined. "We need to destroy that orb!"

"NO!" Convergence snapped. " The orb reached out to you in order to give you cleared insight. You need to bring it to us! It is the only thing that will help us restore long term balance here on Telari and beyond."

"Then," started Cherokee. "We need to get on that ship! and we need a plan for how we can take down those five without killing them."

"What?" asked Nicole.

"I believe that they are victims of Desatyrs' just as we are."

"Guards of Telari," started Convergence, "you can do this! Cherokee, this is the beginning of your destiny!"

CHAPTER TWELVE

THE TABLE WAS too small for five people.

It had once belonged to a family, scratches along its edges, a faint burn mark near the center where a cooking flame had slipped.

The Guards sat around the table in plain clothes, Telarian garments, keeping hidden their armor and power alike.

No one spoke.

Christina rested her forearms on the table, fingers interlaced, eyes steady. Not Cherokee. Christina.

"Okay, team," she said simply. "This is what we're going to do."

Alex leaned back in his chair, footy hooked under a rung. "I'm listening."

"We're going to fight badly."

Nicole blinked. "Come again?"

Christina's eyes met her eyes. "Here me out! No formation. No callouts. No coordination. If it feels wrong, you're doing it right."

Steve frowned as he leaned forward. "That... sounds so wrong and deeply uncomfortable, which means its..."

"Good," interrupted Christina. "The slim guy..." She thought and received. "Vael, he feeds on certainty. On alignment. On intent, so that he can turn it into chaos. We take that certainty away…"

"He'll notice," interrupted Kevin. He then tilted his head, listening to something none of the others could hear.

"Yes," Christina said. "That's the point."

She looked at each of them in turn.

"When I speak again, as Cherokee, he'll come to us. Not to attack. To find a way to cause chaos and then to act on it. This is the power design Desatyr gave him in order to defeat us…" She made a sarcastic laugh. "And it almost worked, but this is why we have to time this perfectly."

"So what do we do once we lure him away?" asked Nicole. "If he confounded us once, he can surely do it again."

Christna nodded an affirmation. "He can, but this time we'll be ready!"

"Your plan?" asked Kevin.

"We put him somewhere he can no longer interfere"!

Alex's jaw tightened, "Mount Sinovia?"

"One way in," Christina said quietly. "One way out. Spell-locked either way."

Shryer exhaled slowly. "A door that only opens if you can magically open it."

Christina nodded. "And Vael can't! He'll be cut off from Desatyr. Being with Convergence will render him unable to do harm. He'll also be safe and protected."

Silence.

Then Nicole smiled. Not wide. Not confident. Determined.

"Alright," she said. "Let's do this wrong!"

***

The village of Hareth Crossing lay under a low greenish gray sky.

The shaytans, it seemed, tried to gather villagers without leadership.

So The Guards automatically knew it was a trap.

The Guards each entered separately.

Altimari arrived first, too fast, skidding to a stop in the open square as if he'd misjudged his landing. He didn't scan rooftops. Didn't wait to confer with his team. He was very haphazard with his approach. Intentionally.

The shaytans started to swarm around him.

Altimari moved in a swift blue blur grabbing a few of their weapons as he left from the area.

Nirvana came in from the opposite direction, boots heavy, cracking stone as she *over committed* to every step, intentionally bringing attention to herself.

As the shaytans turned to face her, she charged in their direction and started picking them up, flinging them far off in various directions.

Altimari jumped up and out of the way as one of the shaytans she threw almost hit him involuntarily.

"Yo, will you watch what you're doin'?" he asked angrily.

"You just stay outta my way!" she yelled back. "You're supposed to be fast...so be fast!"

Kalgorie shifted in quick succession, wolf to hawk to tiger, repeat, never settling, never anchoring as he moved from Shaytan to Shaytan,

"Make up your mind, stupid beast!" yelled Shryer.

Kalgorie morphed into his Telarian form.

"Make me jester!" He then morphed into a large grizzly bear.

Shryer let his illusions fray as lights danced around Kalgorie and confounded him. The edges of the lights blurred. Shapes formed half-way and collapsed again.

Christina walked in last amongst them.

No armor. No glow. Just a woman in a travel cloak, acting as if she could care less about the chaos, until a shaytan reached for her.

"Sleep!" she demanded and the creature fell over effortlessly.

As the space invaders continued to drop in randomly from the beams above, The Guards continued fighting recklessly. Fighting the shaytans and arguing while fighting amongst each other.

Then the air changed.

Vael appeared from a distance near the village well, far enough from the fray but close enough for Christina to spot him right away.

Tall. Thin. Purple skin drawn tight over sharp bone. The red smoke emanating around him soon dissipated.

His presence washed over the square as he drew closer.

Nothing was happening as The Guards continued to fight chaotically.

A shaytan was thrown past him and he watched as it flew by, then turned back to face the chaos he hadn't caused.

Altimari stumbled, but only slightly as he moved about the shaytans.

Nirvana shook her head, annoyed rather than stunned.

"Ugh. I hate this feeling of you always hovering around me, BACK OFF!"

Shryer laughed nervously. "Is it just me, or is Nirvana a little above herself? I thought twins were supposed to stick together?"

Kalgorie morphed into his Telarian form.

"No Shryer It's just you who is above himself! You are confused by your own illusions!"

Vael tilted his head.

There was no cohesion to dampen.

No command to unravel. No unified intent to rot.

For the first time since the vispot orb had remade him, Vael felt... inefficient.

He continued watching.

The Guards then fought Threx when he emerged, sloppy, overlapping, almost careless.

Kalgorie lunged too early, while shifting multiple times.

Shryer threw a hole in which Threx fell in, almost causing Kalgorie in gorilla form to fall in too!

As Threx fell from high above, Nirvana kicked him fifty yards away.

Kalgorie morphed into Telarian form. "Will you watch with your stupid tricks?"

"Poor Kalgorie," started Altimari as he slowed to a stop, "I have to turn into a person before I can talk."

Wait...do I have to change in order to talk? Kalgorie asked himself.

Gaylor popped in behind Nirvana, she instinctively back fisted him, knocking him out.

Then—

Christina spoke.

"I've had Enough!" She put her hand to her chest, risking exposure to her identity to the Shaytons and the image of the gold medallion flipped outward while growing and then flipped backwards until it moved over her and transformed her into her armor. "I'm outta here." She then took to the sky.

"Hey, where do you think you're going?" asked Kalgorie just before transforming into a harpy eagle and flying off after her.

Altimari ran around in a blue blur and knocked out all of the space shaytans left in the village.

He then took off after Kalgorie.

Shryer elevated and encased Nirvana in a gold bubble and they then flew off.

There wasn't one unified word.

But there was a unified action.

The magician had assisted the strong girl in their one directional chase after their leader.

And that was all the unification he needed.

Ignoring his fallen comrades, as he felt his thread snapping back into place, Vael followed The Guards.

***

Cherokee continued flying on as she reestablished connection with her guards, hoping the plan would work.

"Great work," she said. "We do this together!"

Altimari, running just fast enough to stay behind Cherokee, smiled.

They flew towards Humania.

Not running from him but drawing him closer.

"Shryer, prepare the virtual hall!"

While continuing on, Shryer closed his eyes.

"IS IT SAFE FOR YOU TO FLY LIKE WITH YOUR EYES CLOSED?" asked Nirvana.

Shryer just smiled.

***

Vael followed in long lanky strides with a fast pace, quicker than The Guards thought possible since he seemed to only walk slow during their brief previous encounter.

The village blurred into the forest, then a stream and more trees. Then just as he neared Humania, he sensed and then saw The Guards passing by a huge oak tree, but he didn't see them pass by on the other side.

And yet he still sensed them.

Their unifying power and seemingly structured and unbreakable bond called to him even more so.

Vael headed for the large tree and without hesitation, he followed The Guards behind the tree, into a hidden doorway, which immediately closed after he moved through.

***

When Vael stepped out of the portal, the view was dark, but his eyes flipped as he noted the heated outlined silhouettes of the five young adults.

Suddenly the cavern illuminated and Shryer was the first one to grab his attention, standing there with a bright yellow light floating above the pointing finger of his left hand.

The Guards of Telari stood together unified with their right hands over their chest.

The air changed instantly.

Runes ignited along the walls, not flaring, not attacking, *waiting*.

Vael turned in response.

He then looked back at The Guards and smiled as he raised his left hand. Vael then looked at his arm and back at the Guards.

"Yeah bud, that's not gonna work here," said Altimari.

"Convergence, he's still under the influence of the orb?" asked Cherokee.

"And he will be, at least partially if not fully, until you retrieve the orb from Desatyr," replied Convergence.

"Okay Guards," started Cherokee, "let's get back to work! we still have a lot to do before heading for that orb."

Shryer picked up the light off of his finger and tossed it gently towards Vael and it sat suspended in the air in front of him.

One by one The Guards of Telari moved through the portal, appearing to have vanished through the stone wall.

The exit sat there a moment.

Vael reached for it—

And felt the wall.

The cavern sealed.

Vael understood at this moment, he wasn't going anywhere.

****

The Guards emerged miles away, breathless, unshaken, and intact.

Altimari laughed once, sharp and incredulous. "We actually pulled that off."

Shryer bent forward hard. "I hate that I loved that!"

Kalgorie looked back toward the mountain. "He's not gone."

Cherokee nodded. "No. But he's not coming either."

Nirvana crossed her arms, eyes hard. "One down!"

Cherokees, gaze lifted toward the sky, toward the ship, toward the orb, toward the war still ahead.

"Not down," she corrected. "Contained. Now we get ready for the battle!"

The Guards of Telari mentally celebrated as the battlefield now shifted perceivably in their favor.

CHAPTER THIRTEEN

"I'M GOING TO ask you this once," started
Desatyr as he moved steadily around Gaylor
and Threx, both of whom were littered with
bruises and injuries. "Where is Vael?"

The throne room wasn't really used for
interrogation, if Desatyr didn't jail you, or
enslave you, he killed you! He did however feel
more charged when using his throne room in
this way. He used the room at times to ascertain
what occurred with his horde or any creature
considered to be a part of it.

"When I came to my Lord," started Gaylor
as his eyes attempted to follow the Shaytan
Emperor around the room, "Vael, Threx, and
The Guards were all gone."

Desatyrs' eyes cut quickly to Threx. "And
where were you?"

"Tossed aside," started Threx, "put out of
the picture in what looked to be...a chaotic
moment."

Desatyr examined Threxs' words as he soon
stopped walking. "You're saying...they meant to
focus on Vael?"

"What I'm saying is," started Threx angrily
in his rough dialect which sounded like what an
alligator would sound like if it could talk. "The

tall lanky one thrives on chaos and by design, he creates it. When The Guards arrived, they reeked of chaos and confusion, Vael couldn't initiate his objectives with them, so it affected us instead."

"They anticipated what his effect would be on them?" questioned Desatyr. "We need him back! Bring me the animal changer!" barked Desatyr. "We will get Vael's location one way or another."

***

Christina and Steve moved through marketplace, unmasked and unrecognizable to the people of Humania.

Christina grabbed some bread and put it in a felt satchel. "Grab some fruit and veggies for Kevin she said as she pointed to the far left.

Steve stepped back and selected some of the things he knew Kevin liked.

"It's so nice to see the people out doing normal stuff again," said Steve as he rejoined her.

"The Guards of Telari give the people hope and strength," started Christina. "If we do this right, our lives can at least find some normalcy. We all grow tired of running, hiding, or fighting."

"Do you think things will ever go back to normal?" asked Steve.

"That is what we strive for," started Christina as she looked at a few more items. "Sure, we will have The Guards always on stand-by, and if we need to fight to protect our home, we will."

Steve nodded in agreement as without warning, the screams of women and children intruded on the day.

"Well so much for a peaceful day," started Steve as he started to change right there in the market.

Christina stopped him. "Not just yet, let's try to find out who all the players are in this game."

As the shaytans started forcefully moving people, Christina noticed the huntress riding in on her horse, eyes reddened with magic.

"They are wanting to engage us," started Steve. "I say we accommodate them!"

"Yeah, but why here? Of all the villages." She looked around at everyone. "We look like everyone else, how can they know we're..."

A look of realization grew on her face. "Steve, they can sense the power of Convergence! We gotta run! This way!"

The pair started moving with the rest of the crowd

"This way," started Steve as he then pulled Christina into a doorway.

***

Moments later, Cherokee and Shryer came flying in from overhead and soon descended in front of Shanna, the huntress, and Sereth.

Shanna laughed. "Ha, you are here!" she exclaimed as she raised her bow.

Cherokee and Shryer raised their hands in a fighting stance.

Shanna quickly turned her arrow in the direction of a woman and small child cowering in a back corner.

She let go.

Shryer aimed his hands towards the arrow as little bits of yellow sparkles danced around his fingertips.

The arrow morphed into flowers as it hit the woman.

Sereths' eyes started growing brighter and she leaned in and screamed at Cherokee as Cherokee grabbed her head.

Cherokee started to become overrun with emotions. "NO!" she screamed.

Suddenly she saw a vision of *Sereth in a different setting, a lush planet, sky a soft maroon.*

She next saw a vision of Sereth fighting in a war, on the frontline, but it soon became apparent that she was in a military style leadership position, in which she often engaged on the frontline along with the troops she led.

The vision changed, Sereth returned home to her family, a male partner and three children.

The attack happened on her planet, she vowed to serve for Desatyr as he saw fit in exchange for her family to be spared, Desatyr agreed.

Desatyr lied. She doesn't know, the demon consumed her children.

Cherokee knelt as she became overwhelmed with emotions.

Shanna threw down her bow as she engaged Shryer in hand-to-hand combat, a move not expected by the Telarian Guard.

She swung.

He blocked.

She swung again.

He grabbed her arm, twisted behind her head and kicked her behind the left knee, making. her fall to her knees. *Something's wrong*, he thought, *this is way too easy!*

His gut wrenched as a look of realization fell across his face. He suddenly struck Shanna on the back of her head. causing her to pass out.

He then created a doorway perpendicular to Sereth and slid it over towards her, so it could swallow her up.

Cherokee slowly stood up. "Thank you."

"The Huntress could have killed me or you while you were distracted," said Shryer.

"This wasn't about getting rid of us!"

"This was a distraction," agreed Shryer.

Cherokee closed her eyes. "Convergence, I think they may be coming to get Vael"

That is not possible in any way, shape, or form, said Convergence.

"The other Guards!" realized Cherokee.

***

Kevin ascended from the trap door in the ground and sealed it up as he spotted the large reptilian/man hybrid first. He lowered close to the ground like a cat and watched to see what Threx would do next.

Threx was hiding like a snake in the tall grass as he looked on at a herd of deer as they grazed peacefully.

Angered by what was about to happen, Kevin didn't even try to change into his armor. Kevin immediately morphed into the large black panther and sprinted toward Threx as he appeared to be prepping to attack the deer.

The black panther roared as it leapt towards Threx.

Threx turned around and immediately reshaped his head and caught the large cat in his jaws.

The large panther roared/screamed from the pain as Threx threw him five yards to the left.

The panther got up and started towards Threx whose face went back to his normal face.

Threx screeched loudly.

While running, the panther morphed into a large white rhino and charged furiously at the reptile man.

Threx jumped up and flipped over the Rhino as Kevin stopped, morphed into the silverback gorilla, and turned around in just enough time to see Threx land on the ground in front of him.

The gorilla grabbed Threx by his shoulders and slammed him backwards onto the ground.

Threx elongated his left hand sharply, making it look like a green sword, and he rammed it in the gorilla's abdomen.

Kevin, as the gorilla, screamed.

Threx withdrew the sword-like appendage from the gorilla and kicked him, causing him to fly back about twenty feet.

Kevin hit the ground and morphed into a ground hog which funneled his way underground and popped out several yards behind Threx. He then turned into a large gray wolf and started running towards Threx as the reptilian started moving towards him.

The wolf then leapt up and dove into Threx who knocked him to the side with an angry growl.

***

Cherokee and Shryer soon returned to the domicile via a rectangular doorway as they happened on the twins laughing in conversation.

Seeing them their armor, Nicole immediately jumped up.

"Oh," started Cherokee as she developed a look of relief on her face.

"We were caught up in an attack of sorts in Humania, at the marketplace," started Shryer.

"We realized it was some sort of diversion," added Cherokee as she started looking around the domicile unit. "So we wanted to make sure everyone was safe."

She paused.

"Where's Kevin?" Cherokee touched her forehead. "I can't feel him!"

"He wanted to go check on some of his woodland friends in the forest field, by Humania," said Nicole.

"Alex go," started Cherokee as the speedster took off.

Cherokee looked at Nicole. "Kevin may need our help!"

***

Staggering, Threx picked up a large, injured lion by his rear legs and started spinning him around in an attempt to throw him when the

92

lion's tail started morphing first into the tail of a snake which elongated and wrapped around Threxs' waist just as the lizard man let go.

The lion soon fully morphed into a large anaconda which quickly spun itself around Threx until he covered his entire body and his head extended three feet above Threxs' neck.

The anaconda then started squeezing hard.

Every bone in Threxs' body could be heard cracking as the snake looked straight up into the sky.

"ARGH!" screamed Kevin still as the anaconda.

The snake then closed his eyes as he started wiggling loose and as he morphed back into Telarian form, just as the lifeless body of the reptile fell over.

Kevin then started to fall backward as a blue blur appeared behind him, and Altimari caught him, Kevin's body bloodied and bruised.

"I...I had to do it," Kevin said as his eyes closed.

Cherokee soon landed as the yellow bubble Shryer was carrying popped open, allowing Nirvana to drop to the ground.

Shryer soon landed too.

Cherokee covered her mouth and started sobbing.

The physical wounds, those would heal, for certain. The scars that Kevin would have to carry for taking a life, that was a different story altogether.

CHAPTER FOURTEEN

THE UNDERGROUND SPACE smelled faintly of earth and steam.

Shryer's light, left behind by the Telarian magician, hovered near the ceiling, a soft amber glow which never flickered, never warmed, just *existed*.

The light cast long shadows along the stone walls and the uneven floor where bedrolls had been laid out in a loose circle.

Nicole knelt beside Kevin, holding a bowl in both hands.

"Easy," she said quietly. "It's still hot."

Kevin, mostly healed but still in pain, shifted slightly and winced. His torso was bandaged, the wrappings dark in places where blood had soaked through earlier before the healing spell had sealed the worst of it. The rest would take time.

He accepted the bowl with careful hands.

Soup. Thick. Vegetable-heavy. Comfort food, if such a thing still existed.

"You're stuck on baby-sitting duty huh?" he asked softly.

Nicole nodded. "I volunteered."

He took a slow sip and then exhaled.

"Animals don't rush recovery," he said after a moment. "They know better."

Nicole watched him, then sat back on her heels. "You always say stuff like that."

He shrugged. "They taught me."

She hesitated, then said, "Alex and I... we didn't get taught much after the first strike."

Kevin looked up.

"The first shaytan incursion," she continued. "We were kids. Parents didn't make it out. I assume the first time it happened; they were feeling us out...sampling...maybe that's why they came back later...they knew how easy it would be to take our world."

Kevin nodded once. "Or so they thought...I was younger. Don't remember my parents clearly. Just that, one day they were gone, and I felt lost. Shadow found me just as the aliens did and he saved my life. That's why I like taking his form, the panther because I am reminded of how brave he was. With regards to my parents, it's easier for me to believe they were taken, rather than believing I was just left behind."

Nicole glanced at him. "What did you do?"

"I just walked, hoping I would catch up to them when I was found," he said. "I thought I was losing my mind a talking panther until I realized all of the animals were talking to me. Either they understood me or I understood them, at the time it didn't matter, my life was saved."

A faint smile tugged at his mouth. "The animals, they don't ask where you came from.

Or why you're broken. You just exist with them. You always belong."

Nicole swallowed. "You don't eat animal matter?"

Kevin nodded.

"Some animals do," she started, so why did you choose not to.

"It was a personal choice," Kevin replied. He grunted and shifted again. "I never wanted or felt the need to take a life. Even the animals who do respected my choice and it was never a problem."

"Do they consider you their king?"

"No, and I have always respected them more than that to try and impose such a tale."

"Good answer," she said truly impressed.

"What was it like growing up with a twin brother?"

"Alex is my heart," she smiled fondly. I'll never tell him that of course..."

They both laughed.

Kevin winced a little.

"Hurts huh?"

Kevin nodded. "Especially when I laugh."

"When our parents were first taken, three of the Shaytans had my mom and I was fighting them and winning but then I heard my mom tell Alex to get me out of there...and he did."

"That made you mad?"

"I struck him and he didn't wake up for about three days."

"Ouch."

"I regretted it as soon I struck him. Ww were found by a farmer family, and we stayed with them until we were old enough to fend for ourselves."

"But growing up," she continued, "Alex was always the annoying and playful one...he always dreamed of visiting the planet our ancestors immigrated from?"

"Really?"

She nodded.

"You ever think of visiting Earth one day?" he asked.

"I never think about it being as we don't have the technology."

Kevin smiled a little. "We take that ship, we'll have it!"

They both laughed.

He again winced.

"If you go, I'll go," she said.

Kevin smiled. "It's a date!"

They sat in silence after that, the light humming softly above them.

***

Christina stood near the edge of the temporary shelter; hands braced on a stone table etched with old markings.

Alex paced, slower than usual.

Steve leaned against the wall, arms crossed, eyes half-closed in thought.

"We can't stay here," Christina said.

It wasn't panic. It wasn't fear.

It was fact.

Alex stopped pacing. "Because of their ability to detect us?"

"Yes," Christina replied. "The magic from Convergence leaves a scent. Even when we don't act. Even when we hide."

Steve opened his eyes. "So fixed locations are liabilities." He sighed. "We really need to get that orb!"

Christina nodded. "Every hour we remain in one place, the risk compounds."

Alex ran a hand through his hair. "So we move."

"Constantly," Steve said. "Illusions won't hold forever."

Christina straightened. "We become nomads until we defeat Desatyr. No center. No pattern. No expectation of safety."

Alex looked at her. "That's not living."

"No," she said quietly. "It's surviving long enough to finish this. We can still get to wherever we're needed to protect our people, so that's a plus."

Steve tilted his head. "We rotate rest zones. Underground. Ruins. Old Telarian conduits. We move before Convergences' echoes build."

Alex nodded slowly. "And when they try to grab us again?"

"They fail," Christina said.

"And if they don't?" Asked Alex.

"We make an understanding amongst the five of us, that no one person is bigger than the mission to save our planet."

The weight of that hung between the three of them.

"We do what we can to keep each other safe, but the ultimate goal is to get that vispot orb from Desatyr and destroy his army."

"Destroy?" queried Steve.

Christina nodded her head in the affirmative and walked around with her arms folded. "I am able to calculate multiple possibilities of a variety of situations, but after what happened with Kevin, after what I witnessed about Sereth...I don't see any other way to do this."

Steve nodded in agreement.

"Okay," Alex agreed.

"This war doesn't give us time to grieve," she said. "But I am sure we will pay that debt later."

***

Sereth sat alone in her quarters.

The room was dim, metallic, and orderly, too orderly. There were no personal artifacts. There was no comforts from home. Just a narrow sleeping platform and a console built into the far wall.

Her head throbbed.

The images of her past replayed over and over in her head again. That wasn't how her powers were supposed to work. Being that she projected her emotions onto a powerful opponent who was also an empath had unexpected consequences...the replacing of her memories through images she could not recollect.

Every time she closed her eyes, they came again, sleep would feel haunted to her and she wasn't sure why, she recognized no one from the visions, yet she saw herself in every one of them.

Increasingly, the images came in bits and fragments now. She recognized them not as visions, but as memories.

A sky, soft maroon. Three small hands in hers. Laughter, hers and those of children. A male partner, caressing her, holding her, kissing her. The five of them bonding together.

She pressed her fingers to her temples. Even though she wasn't sure where they came from, the memories made her feel warm inside.

"No," she whispered.

The console chimed softly as it activated. She hadn't yet touched it.

Sereth started to recognize her own distress.

She left her quarters, unable to rest.

Desatyr was angered by the death of Threx, but he didn't seem to care.

Why do I care? she asked herself.

New emotions flowed through her every time she saw the memories.

She found the ships central archive computer.

She started thinking. *I can project emotions onto living beings and access data if they feel. Can I just touch this machine and access information?*

She touched the console, the red light glowed where she connected.

A beep sounded.

"Access: planetary records New Axion," she said.

To her surprise, the screen flickered.

Her home world's designation soon appeared.

Then the status.

ORDERED EXTINCTION CONFIRMED.

NO SURVIVORS DETECTED.

Sereth stared and her emotions seemed to stagnate.

She scrolled through the data, combat logs, energy signatures, consumption patterns. That last one confused her, and she wasn't sure why that was there.

The one thing she noticed was that Desatyr's signature was everywhere.

Her breath came in shallow gasps.

A flash back.

I know of you," started Desatyr. "You are a leader, a valiant warrior, it would cause me slight discomfort to waste someone like you."

She kneeled before him. " I will do your bidding; I just ask that you spare my family."

"It is...a deal. I will imprison you until I can figure out how to best utilize your skill set."

The flashback ended.

"They were supposed to live," she remembered as she covered her mouth and as tears started pouring down. "Maybe they're on this ship," she said out loud and to herself.

The screen did not respond.

She stood there, knees trembling.

The truth unknown and just as questionable, as ice is cold.

Somewhere deep within her, something started to crack.

She needed to find the truth and for the first time since the vispot orb rebirthed her, Sereth did not think of her orders.

She thought of her family.

CHAPTER FIFTEEN

GADASCAR WAS UNDERSEIGED and the shaytans did not hold back. They captured the Telarians however they could, using ropes, nets, arrows.

Desatyr's orders were simple, no further use of the decomposition cannons as the continued application of enemy disintegration eliminated the possibility of capture.

No capture meant, meant no slaves.

It also meant no food rations.

Capture and let no guard interfere.

Altimari was closest. The blue blur zipped into Gadascar and quickly loosened netting.

He untied ropes.

He collected arrows as they were being fired and threw, redirected them back at random shaytans.

Shanna the Huntress rode in on her white stallion.

Gaylor popped in. He saw the one they called Altimari and he growled.

Altimari saw him too and sped up, racing ahead of his manifestations.

He saw the first sign of the red smoke appearing and moved quickly, catching Gaylor's

face with his fist and then his back with an
elbow.

Gaylor fell to the ground and popped out of
sight.

Altimari kept moving at the same speed
when he saw the red smoke start to show up
again.

Gaylor popped fully in as Altimari leg swept
him down and then grabbed his arm and swung
him into a tree.

Gaylord hit the ground and then growled
furiously. He then looked down and grabbed a
hand full of dirt and then popped out of site.

Altimari kept moving and spotted the red
cloud forming near a tree to his left.

He moved quickly.

He grabbed and a split second too late he
realized he wasn't reaching for Gaylor as the
space popper reappeared behind him and
jabbed four arrows in his right leg.

Altimari screamed as Gaylor popped out of
site and quickly reappeared and jammed arrows
in his left arm.

Altimari swung.

POP.

He missed.

POP.

Arrows jammed in his other leg. Altimari
fell hard on that one.

Cherokee flew in and was carrying Nirvana
telepathically. They both landed.

Nirvana ran for Altimari as the huntress
fired multiple arrows at her and they
ricochetted off of her.

Cherokee swung her hand and knocked the huntress off her horse and into a tree.

Gaylor picked up the screaming Altimari and...

POP.

They were gone.

Nirvana fell to her knees. "NOOOO!"

Cherokee moved her hand around in a circle and put all the shaytans to sleep at once, but a yellow light came down from one of the ships and picked up the huntress, her horse, and the remaining shaytans in the blink of an eye.

The ship then took off and was soon gone.

***

The lights in the little underground cavern seemed brighter this time.

Steve held his hands up as Kevin punched them in rapid succession, switching from left to right.

Kevin then did a light trot type of dance with his feet going back and forth. He then, keeping his right foot flat on the floor and then leaning back, he started kicking Steves' right and left hand in alternating succession.

Kevin then lowered his foot and started the trot again.

Steve started shaking the pain out of his hands. "Well, someone's getting better."

Steve, we have a problem, get to Gadascar. He heard Cherokee's voice say.

"I'll be back Kevin, Cherokee needs me."

"I should go to," Kevin started

"Focus on getting better," Steve said holding
his hand in a stop position. "I don't know yet
what the situation is, "be back soon!"

A square doorway opened in front of Steve
and he stepped through.

***

The doorway opened in Gadascar and
Shryer stepped out seeing Nirvana crying in
Cherokee's arms.

"What happened?" he asked.

Cherokee looked up first. "They took Alex!"

"What?!"

"We have to get him back," started Nirvana.

"And we will," Cherokee started, "but we all
agreed that we need to finish the mission first."

"What?" asked Nirvana as she pulled back
from Cherokee. "They will kill him!"

"Nicole," started Cherokee as she looked
Nirvana in the eyes, "I swear on my life, we will
get him back!"

Cherokee looked up towards the sky.

Shryer touched Nirvana on her shoulder.

"I must continue to believe, that everything
will be okay," Cherokee said.

***

Desatyr stood inside of the prisoner's cell,
smiling nefariously at the Telarian who was
strung up, with his garb torn off, blood dripping
from his body still from when they yanked the
arrows out of his skin.

He sniffed him and smiled again. "You have
a familiar scent, I've tasted something like you
before, a long time ago."

106

Alex didn't react, hurting and weakened from the last attack.

"When I'm done with you," started Desatyr, "You're going to wish you perished on that battlefield. But first...SERETH!"

Sereth stepped forward. "Cause this creature tremendous pain, like only you can."

"Yes, my lord," Sereth replied.

"And when he cannot take anymore and starts begging for you to stop, find out where Vael is and ask him how they are hiding him from us...then end him!"

"Yes, my lord!"

Desatyr smiled and he left out of the prisoner's cell.

Feeling defeated and stuck in pain, Alex immediately realized that nothing was hurting anymore.

Sereth was staring when he finally lifted his eyes to her.

She didn't make a sound at first, but then she took her left hand and touched his chin.

"Don't say a word, I am taking away your pain as your body heals, but I'm gonna need some assistance from you."

CHAPTER SIXTEEN

SERETH SAT UP from her bed and stayed for a moment. Her respirations were increased and she knew before she got started, she had to slow them down.

Then another flashback.

Sereth placed a finger in the hand of a very small child.

The flashback ended.

She stood up and looked in the mirror.

Another flashback.

A small child laughed.

The flashback ended.

Sereth looked at herself a little longer than she intended. She then turned from the mirror and walked away.

She soon left out of the quarters as the door slid open upon her approach.

After leaving out, she turned left and her door slid closed.

Emotionally absent and with purposeful strides, she made her way around the ship as she headed to the prisoner's cell.

She wondered how she could find out where her family was being kept without alerting the emperor she was looking for him.

Upon her arrival, the prisoner looked up at her dolefully.

Desatyr turned to her and smiled. "I knew I was correct in my decision to retain you...you are doing excellent work!"

"Thank you, my lord!"

"I have the huntress and some of my troops following up on the leads you extracted from this one. I will alert you once we have Vael and you will kill him!"

"My lord, might I seek permission to kill him slowly, piece by piece, I think I might be able to learn some secrets related to The Guards of Telari and Convergence."

"Sereth you've become increasingly ambitious of late and I must say...I rather like this part of you." He then turned to leave. "Have at him!"

Desatyr then left out the cell.

Sereth walked over towards Altimari. "Now...where were we?"

Altimari managed to look at her a little, concern growing as he wondered what was next.

***

Gaylor stood in the weapons shed and armed himself with a whip and a dagger. He then adjusted his garment top as he made his way to Desatyr's throne room.

"My lord, you wanted to see me?"

"Yes Gaylor," he started as he sat on his throne and looked downward toward his general. "You have done me great justice by catching the one they call, Altimari."

"Thank you, my lord!"

"The end is nye," Desatyr started. "Once we have Vael back, we will see the destruction of The Guards, once and for all. Then, we will return to our initial plan of harvesting this planet of its resources and of its inhabitants."

"Speaking of which my lord," started Gaylor as he glanced over at the pulsating red vispot orb and then back up at the demon. "I understand you intend to send the Huntress and some of your troops down to secure Vael?"

"Your concern?"

"Once the guards realize that their comrade is not present for the exchange," I believe they will prevent the collection of your chaos bringer." Gaylor then bowed. "Please allow me to collect him once the conflict ensues."

Desatyr smiled. He then nodded in the affirmative as Gaylor stood up.

"Thank you, my Lord!"

"Gaylor?" started Desatyr. "You pull this off and you will be greatly rewarded!"

Gaylor nodded and turned and left out of the throne room, smiling.

***

Nirvana was running through the forest of Humania, Vael, unconscious, thrown over her shoulders. As she approached the wide river of Sh'nook, she braced herself and made sure she held firm onto Vael as she leapt high up and over the river with grace.

She landed firmly. She then took off running again.

She soon slowed to a stop when she saw the Huntress and her band of shaytans.

110

She held her grip on the still unconscious Vael as she looked around.

"You're alone," started the huntress, "I guess it's safe to assume no one else was amenable to the exchange?"

"Where's Altimari?" asked Nirvana.

"Vael first!" demanded Shanna.

"Nirvana wait," started Cherokee as her and Shryer soon landed behind her. "This is not the way!"

"Spare me the bull shit Cherokee, he's not your brother."

One of the shaytans started to raise his bow and arrow to shoot and Shanna raised her hand to signal him to hold.

"Wait," she said quietly. "This is amusing!"

"Enough of this," started Shryer, "Cherokee you're too soft on her!"

Shryer threw a ball of light in Nirvana's direction which started to grow on its way to her.

She dropped Vael to the ground and prepared to stop the huge ball as Cherokee astral projected herself over the ball and drew the light into her astral self. "Guards that's enough!" exclaimed Cherokee in astral form. "Nirvana, I said we're not doing this and that's final!"

Suddenly, in a flash of red smoke, Gaylor appeared standing behind Nirvana!

Cherokee's astral formed snapped back to her physical body as Gaylor picked up Vael.

"NOOO!" she yelled as Gaylor smiled at her
and then looked at Shanna. "Desatyr has no
time for games!"

POP.

He was gone.

Shryer screamed angrily.

Nirvana tore a tree out of the ground and
threw it at the shaytans and Shanna laughed.

A yellow light from above beamed down and
removed Shanna and her shaytans from the
battlefield.

Nirvana looked over to Cherokee who
looked over to Shryer.

"Shryer," she started angrily, "Take us to
Convergence!"

Shryer drew a line of light straight down in
front of his torso and then one perpendicular to
that line, forming four perfect right angles with
a central intersection. He then spun the cross
around until the lines blurred and the trio were
all close in proximity in darkness.

Then a light appeared.

"Well?" asked Convergence as Cherokee
slowly looked up.

Nirvana and Shryer looked at each other
and then ahead at Cherokee who smiled. "Part
one worked!"

"Excellent!" proclaimed Convergence.

"How is our guest, by the way?" asked
Cherokee as she looked over at Vael who
appeared to be amused."

"I think the vispot orb is losing its grip on
our guest," started Convergence, "He seems to
be starting to understand."

Vael forged a smile on his otherwise expressionless face. "Thank...you!" he said.

Cherokee nodded. "Now, it's up to the others," she said as she looked upward.

***

Sereth walked out of the throne room after she learned of Vael's return to the fold. Gaylor was promised a reward, Shanna smiled in jubilation, Vael was tucked away in his quarters resting as she headed back to her prisoner with orders to execute him.

Again, a flash back hit her.

Mommy, you promised you wouldn't hurt the good ones!

The flash ended.

"I promise baby, I even go to the front lines myself to make sure my soldiers are mindful," she said out loud and to herself.

Sereth gasped as she covered her mouth and a tear descended from her eye. Either the vispot orb was losing its grip or it was intentionally letting go because she was remembering more.

***

In Vael's quarters, the being inhaled deeply as if he was holding his breath. He then slowly sat up and moved over to the mirror and looked in and for a split second, he didn't recognize the face.

Then a flashback.

"Convergence said I can morph into any living creature," started Kalgorie, "so I should be able to look like him."

"Try it," said Cherokee.

Kalgorie slowly morphed first into a snake and then transitioned into an exact replica of Vael.

"By the trinity, that worked!" proclaimed Nirvana.

"Only thing is," started Kalgorie, "If I fall unconscious for any reason, I may not be able to hold form."

"Then we'll create a spell to lock this as your baseline form while keeping your other abilities intact," started Shryer. "I'm also gonna put you in a deep sleep spell which will release when your inertia has been still for over an hour."

"Find Sereth when it's safe, free Altimari, and get the orb. Once you have possession of it, we can confront Desatyr and this war will be over."

"Just don't die," added Nirvana as she kissed him on the cheek.

The flashback ended.

Kalgorie as Vael rubbed the side of his face. "Just...don't...die! Riiight!"

CHAPTER SEVENTEEN

SERETH STOOD OUTSIDE the prisoner's cell longer than necessary, but she was cautious not to show any signs of hesitation to any of the shaytans.

The door had not opened yet. The shaytan emperor had been clear with his orders.

End him.

She rested her palm against the cold metal wall and closed her eyes.

A memory surfaced uninvited via flashback.

Small hands. Three of them. Warm. Trusting.

The flashback ended.

She inhaled sharply.

"No," she whispered.

The door slid open.

Altimari hung where he had been left, arms bound, head lowered, breath shallow but steady. He slowly lifted his eyes when he sensed her presence.

"You've returned?" he asked hoarsely.

Sereth stepped inside. The door sealed behind her with a soft hiss.

Desatyr's voice echoed in her mind.

Pain. Information. Execution.

She moved close to him.

Altimari smiled a little.

"Why do you keep fighting the shaytans?" she asked quietly.

Altimari blinked. "Because it matters."

"To whom?"

"To everyone who lives, to everyone who still desires to live. It is our promise to our people!"

Her jaw tightened.

"I was promised something once, a promise for my family to live if I served," she said, almost to herself. "A lie wrapped in mercy."

Altimari studied her face. Really looked at her.

"You've been remembering them," he said.

It wasn't a question.

Her breath hitched.

"I don't know who them are," she replied. "Only that they feel...of me... right."

She turned away from him, pacing once, twice.

"If I were to do his bidding and let you die," she continued, "the war continues unchanged. A coward disguised as an emperor goes on to destroy multitudes more!"

"And if you don't?" Altimari asked.

Sereth stopped.

"That," she said, "is where the real question lies, for I am not certain which path is actually the most appropriate. Staying subservient to the Devil I know..."

She moved back to him and pressed her fingers against the restraints.

"...or aligning myself with the ones I don't."

The metal *softened*.

Altimari's eyes widened as he felt the restraints weaken.

"I cannot free you," she said quickly. "Not yet. Not without consequences."

"You helped us out once, that was huge. Don't do anything else that will jeopardize your life." he said.

Sereth leaned closer, lowering her voice.

"My life truly ended when I learned the fate of my home, and most likely, my family. Desatyr believes I am breaking you," she said. "And tonight... I will give him what he expects, one last time."

She straightened and raised her hand again, this time directing her power *away* from Altimari, as he was fully healed.

The pain of torture would now sound authentic to those listening, but they would be from her.

She screamed with an inflected voice sounding masculine.

She forced the scream from her throat, flooding the corridor with the sound of agony which was not actually happening to the prisoner, but which came from her own grief and loss.

The ship's systems registered it.

In the throne room, the vispot orb pulsed.

Altimari stared at her in stunned silence.

"Remember this of the many sacrifices I made for you when the time comes. Keep fighting the good fight," Sereth said, voice shaking. "They will come to inspect your body soon, you must be more swift than you've ever been at that time. You will not be afforded another chance."

Altimari nodded.

"Thank you Sereth."

She nodded.

Then she deactivated the field and exited the cell.

Outside, she steadied herself as Desatyr's voice echoed in her head.

Is he broken?

"It is done, my lord," Sereth said over the com on the wall.

"Well done Sereth!" he replied.

She told him a lie.

She smiled for the first time since the time of her planets' attack. Lying to Desatyr felt like breathing.

CHAPTER EIGHTEEN

DESATYR WALKED AROUND the throne room after getting Sereths' message feeling renewed. One of the Guards of Telari had been terminated, Vael was standing before him, looking renewed and refreshed, and Gaylor had restored his faith in the choosing of his generals, especially him.

"Gaylor, I suspect The Guards will attempt an attack since we have Vael and we have not returned their soldier, so I need you to prepare an army and we will clear out the villages first. With Vael by your side, we can collect the rest of the guards when they attempt to interfere!"

"Yes, my lord," Gaylor started to leave but then he turned back to Desatyr. "My lord, should we put the vispot orb in more...protective housing, I sense it may become a product of procurement."

Vael listened closely.

Desatyr smirked. "I had the same concern Gaylor," started Desatyr. "You needn't worry, I have it encased in an invisible electric shield, if any hand other than my own reaches for it, they will be evaporated immediately."

"Very good my lord!"

Gaylor then left out of the throne room and the second hiss from the door informed Vael that the door was closed.

Desatyr continued to walk around Vael. "Vael I need you to escort my verifiers to the cell where the one called Altimari is kept. In the event that he is still alive, I'll need you there to slow him down..."

A melting liquid sound interrupted Desatyr as the arm of a large silverback guerilla wrapped around his neck, causing the shaytan emperor to attempt to remove the arm unsuccessfully."

"Go to sleep," started Kalgorie in a deep quiet rough gorilla voice. "Go to sleep, Go to sleep my...little baby!"

Desatyr started slapping Kalgorie's arm faster.

"Close your eyes, close them tight, go to sleep, go to sleep!"

Desatyr passed out and Kalgorie dropped him on the floor and the liquid sound assisted him with morphing into a replica of the shaytan emperor himself.

"I sure hope this works!" started Kalgorie as Desatyr as he reached into the stand and slowly grabbed the orb.

As he pulled his hand back and held the vispot orb, he breathed a sigh of relief. He then removed a waist held satchel from the unconscious emperor and placed the vispot orb inside as he reverted back into Vael.

Kalgorie as Vael then smiled. "You know, you really shouldn't walk around in circles when you're talking. You might miss something!"

The door to the Throne room soon hissed open causing Vael to look on surprised.

Sereth soon entered the throne room.

Vael tied the satchel to his waist and slowly walked past her and smiled. "Slight change in plans, but he's all yours anyway."

Sereth nodded.

Vael left out.

The throne room door hissed closed.

Sereth moved over Desatyr and placed her hands on his head. "I'm looking for four sets of emotions in particular," she said as she touched him.

***

Vael made his way around the ship his gait a little faster than normal.

From across the bridge, Gaylor noticed his speed, a habit he picked up as a space popper, always calculating the moves of others. Since Desatyr changed Vael to suit his own needs, the ungracefully lean creature has always ambulated in the same manner, with a slow awkward gait, then he thought about it and remembered that he did give chase to the guards right before he was caught.

He observed the creature until he was no longer in sight. Vael's blank facial expression was the same, nothing else seemed different about him. *Maybe I better ask Desatyr if Vael is truly ready for another mission,* he thought.

***

Vael soon located the cell holding Altimari when he felt the tap on his shoulder. He turned around and saw two shaytans standing behind him.

"We was told you were gonna get us when we was ready to check the body?"

Kalgorie as Vael realized he had almost forgotten about that; He waved ahead and allowed the shaytans to touch the wall and enter first.

As soon as they walked in, the door hissed closed behind them and the two shaytans were standing in front of Vael as one of them held a shocker probe up in preparation to electrocute the body for verification.

"This my favorite part," laughed one of the shaytans as the other laughed right along with him. "You cans eat the meat right off the bone after this shock! On the count of three, Ones...Two..."

Vael clunked their heads together, causing them to fall out.

Altimari picked his head up and jumped down since Sereth softened the metal so he could break free. "Cuttin' that close to the wire my friend weren't you?"

Vael said, "I was trying to come in without them."

"What now?" asked Altimari.

"Shryer said the vispot orb wants to leave," started Kalgorie as Vael. "We just have to tell it where to go!"

"How do we do that?" asked Altimari.

"Stand close to me," said Vael as the door to the cell hissed open.

"Vael you done yet..."started Gaylor as he looked at the bodies on the floor and then over at Vael and Altimari."

Vael held the vispot orb and said, "To Chrystal and Sorrie."

Gaylor growled and headed towards them but then they vanished in a puff of red smoke.

***

As Sereth screamed while holding Desatyr's head, with him screaming at the same time, he suddenly stopped screaming as his eyes opened wide and he quickly grabbed Sereth by the neck as he stood up.

She appeared unphased that he was holding her up off the ground by her neck as the tears rolled down her cheeks.

"As you have done for me," she started in a raspy voice, "I took what was precious from you!"

Desatyr screamed and quickly twisted his wrist, breaking her neck and tossing her across the room where her lifeless body hit the wall and fell to the floor.

A second later Gaylor popped into the throne room.

Desatyr turned angrily toward Gaylor. "This wretched planet is more trouble than it's worth! Forget the inhabitants, recall all troops from reconnaissance of the planet, and prepare to engage the molecular decomposition cannon on this planet."

"My lord, it will take seven days to prepare the cannon and move the ship far enough to not be affected,"

"Understood," replied Desatyr. "Now do it!"

CHAPTER NINETEEN

THE GUARDS OF TELARI, all five of them, all stood in the cavern along with Vael who watched with amusement as Kalgorie passed the red vispot orb to Cherokee.

Kalgorie and Altimari stood with their team in full armor, thankful that they were able to not only escape the warship, but to take the sacred orb from the shaytan emperor.

The vispot orb glowed brightly in Cherokee's hands as a since of familiarity and belonging washed over her when all of a sudden red smoke poured out of Vael's body and into the orb.

The vispot orb then ascended upward until neither it, nor its trailing red light, was in sight.

"Kalgorie, did you feel a strange sensation too when you were holding the orb?" asked Cherokee.

"The only thing I felt was relief when I took it away from Desatyr," replied Kalgorie.

***

As she was moving through the corridors, Shanna felt a strange sensation wash over her as she looked around the ship. She knew where she was, she knew how she had gotten there, and she knew what she had done under the influence of Desatyr.

She turned around in the opposite direction from where she was headed and rushed to get Ion, her white stallion.

She reached the stable where Ion was located and released him as the horse whinnied and neighed excitedly upon seeing her.

"Shh boy," she said calmly as she patted the nose of the stallion. "I think it's time we make our exit. Better our fate end here on this world than go on living with the enemy of all!"

after untying Ion they made their way out of the ships stable and headed down a hall where they quickly found the transporter pad.

A shaytan approached her as she placed Ion on the pad.

"Stay boy," she said as she turned and faced the shaytan.

"Shanna you can't be..."

Shanna quickly took her bow from behind her back, through it over the shaytans' head, pulled him close, lifted the bow and kicked him back against the wall, causing him to pass out.

She then ran over to the pad and typed onto the keyboard.

A beep sounded as she ran over to the transporter pad.

Another beep.

A pause.

Then a final beep.

The bright light then shone on them, and they vanished from off the ship.

***

"I am free," said Vael. "Finally free!"

"Look who can talk," started Shryer.

"Yes," started Vael, "On my home world, before the shaytan emperor attacked, I was one of a group of archivists, tasked with keeping records of major events occurring with, to, and on our world."

"Maybe you can go back and finish your work?" suggested Nirvana.

"You would not know this," started Vael, "but once Desatyr attacks a planet, he rarely leaves anything behind unless he plans to make it a base station."

"He destroyed your planet?" asked Altimari. "He attacked our home once before, years ago."

"Then you were living on borrowed time, as he came back to claim this world as his own."

"And now that he knows he can't take it and has lost the orb," started Cherokee, "It's only a matter of time before he decides to destroy the planet."

"In a matter of speaking you are correct," started Vael. "They have a weapon, similar to the prototypes they used upon arrival when they want to scare your people into submission."

"The destabilizing cannons?" asked Cherokee.

"This one is much larger of course and sits upon their warship. It takes time, six to eight days to be exact, in order to fully charge, but it also requires the warship to elevate in a stepwise manner to be able to break the planet's gravitational field once the weapon detonates."

"And you know this how?" asked Kalgorie.

"Have you not paid attention young one?" asked Vael. "I observe and mentally record everything."

"Vael, you're welcome to stay on our planet, "started Cherokee, "we could use someone with your skills and talent."

Vael nodded.

"So what do we do to prolong the inevitable," asked Nirvana.

Cherokee smiled. "Well, they need to charge the weapon and elevate the ship," started Cherokee. "So I think the most logical explanation would be...to take down their mother ship."

"That would flood our planet with shaytans," said Altimari. "Wouldn't it?"

"Shaytans stuck on our planet?" asked Cherokee. "Or our planet reduced to atoms? Pick your poison."

"Okay," started Shryer, "but that would mean Desatyr will be down here with us too."

"I guess we'll cross that bridge when we get to it," said Cherokee.

CHAPTER TWENTY

THE WARSHIP HAD begun to rise. Not noticeably at first but when they could see the flock of passing geese flying under it, they were certain it had moved higher.

Kalgorie sought confirmation from one of his flying friends, a falcon who frequently visited with him, even before he became one of Telaris' Guards.

"How much has it ascended?" asked Cherokee as she looked up at the mighty war vessel.

"Not enough to warrant alarm," responded Kalgorie, "it is currently around sixty thousand feet above ground level."

Vael saw it.

"They are adjusting elevation in increments," he said quietly, standing beside Cherokee at the ridge overlooking Gadascar. "A preparatory arc. When the cannon fires, they must be beyond the planet's gravitational pull."

"How long?" asked Altimari.

"Six days at minimum," Vael replied. "Seven to be safe."

"I'm sure they could care less about our safety," replied Altimari.

"Their safety," corrected Kalgorie. "Their safety."

The sky hummed faintly above them.

Cherokee turned to the gathering Telarians below. There were a multitude of families consisting of men, women, elders, and children. Everyone, including the children were clutching woven satchels, taking with them food and other essential necessities

Fear was written across many of their faces, but there were also some with hope.

"They will destroy this world," she said plainly. "Unless we act."

Murmurs rippled through the crowd.

"And you expect us to follow him?" one of the elders asked, pointing at Vael.

Vael did not flinch.

Cherokee nodded in the affirmative as she stepped forward.

"Neither Vael nor Shanna are under the vispot orb's control any longer," she said. "And if we do not trust those who have learned the harshness of the shaytans firsthand, then we are doomed to suffer the same fate as the people of the worlds Desatyr has already destroyed."

Silence.

Vael spoke carefully. "Shanna and I both know their reconnaissance patterns. How they do their atmospheric scans. We can lead you beyond their sweep range, and we promise to keep you safe."

Nirvana crossed her arms. "He stayed with the Trinity while we retrieved the orb."

The murmuring restarted and then softened.

"You mean he was with Convergence?" asked a slim man from the crowd.

"He stayed there as Desatyrs' poisoned influence left his body," replied Shryer.

"He like most of us," started Cherokee, "has loss so much. He is giving back as penance for his wrong doings under influence which was not his own, and he wishes to become Telarian."

Cherokee lifted her chin. "Upon Vael's signal, Convergence will open passage to the highlands of Arenthis. Far beyond the warship's trajectory. You evacuate now."

Shryer drew lines of light into the air.

Doorways shimmered into open portals.

Vael raised his arm. "Follow me," he said.

Altimari leaned in toward Nirvana. "Yeah, he might want to stop doing that raising the arm thing."

She did an overexaggerated laughed and punched him lightly in the arm.

"Ow," said Altimari.

Families began stepping through after Vael.

Altimari moved quickly among them, assisting the elderly when needed.

Shanna and Ion stood apart, watching quietly, bow slung across her back. Monitoring the rear and then following them in.

As the last of the civilians disappeared into safety, Cherokee turned back to the sky.

"Now," she said softly, "we take the sky from them."

CHAPTER TWENTY-ONE

THE GUARDS STRUCK at dusk.

The shaytan mothership hovered over Gadascar, its occupants, quiet, believing that The Guards were merely being passive after winning their last battle.

Cherokee flew towards the huge ship holding Nirvana by her wrists.

She then flew up above the hull and let Nirvana go.

Nirvana immediately struck the rear thrusters first.

As soon as she hit them the alarms started blaring.

Three loud beeps sounded. "

Rear thrusters compromised, descent initiated," started a computerized female voice."

The ship then made a series of hissing sounds as it started preparing to lower in elevation."

Nirvana smiled as she ran to the edge of the ship and jumped.

A yellow bubble soon encircled her and her velocity started decreasing.

She laughed. "Shryer, I could've made that!"

"Today's not the day for us to prove or test that hypothesis," he said as he moved into her field of view.

***

Inside the massive ship, the alarms continued to ring out as Desatyr made his rare appearance onto the bridge.

"What's going on?" he snarled?

A shaytan turned from his viewer while pointing at it.

"It looks like one of The Guards of Telari has taken out our rear thrusters!"

"How did this happen?" Desatyr asked angrily. "Where's my perimeter team?"

The shaytan started shivering. "You ordered a full retreat back to Shay!"

Desatyr picked up the whimpering shaytan.

"Why would I order a full retreat when my lead vessel is still hovering above this wretched planet?"

"A valid question my lord," started the shaytan, "many of us was wondering the same..."

Being thrown across the bridge and into a wall interrupted the shaytan who fell unconscious upon impact.

"Someone recall my fleet...NOW!"

"Ten Thousand feet A - G - L," announced the computerized voice, "please brace for impact!"

***

The Guards stood by and watched as the large mothership soon touched the planets' surface with a thunderous crash, even though the descent was controlled.

A tear opened near the rear of the ship.

Altimari saw his opening and breached first, blue streak slicing through the warship's outer hull before additional alarms could register.

Shryer followed with a beam of concentrated light, forming entry corridors into the ship.

Nirvana entered, disorienting shaytan sentries with a series of quick blows, one with a punch up to the ceiling and then with a hard crash to the floor.

Kalgorie moved like memory itself, guiding them through mechanical arteries and weapon chambers, areas he learned from his brief time upon the war ship.

Cherokee landed on the hull moments later. She then entered one of Shryers' manufactured doorways.

She didn't announce herself. She didn't need to. He would soon find out who she is.

The shaytans on board started firing but a blue blur simply zipped by and disarmed them.

"Now, now," started Altimari, "let's stop getting dependent on these!"

Altimari then found Gaylor.

The two circled in the metallic space.

"You move well again," Gaylor sneered.

"You still teleport sloppily," Altimari answered.

They clashed.

Speed against spatial distortion.

Gaylor popped, reappeared, struck, but Altimari anticipated every emergence, blocking each punch, missing each foot from an attempted disorienting kick. Altimari kept adapting and moved with Gaylor's rhythm.

He finally caught Gaylor mid-pop and hurled him across the chamber.

Gaylor hit the wall hard, broken but alive.

Altimari did not finish him.

He turned away and that was his mistake as the space popper quickly vanished.

Steve noticed a slight puff of red smoke behind Altimari and quickly threw up a metal sheet, dividing the smoke in half as Gaylor appeared, eyes widened and seemingly petrified as his body fell from either side of the sheet just as Altimari turned around and witnessed the site.

"EW!" he exclaimed as he looked over at Shryer who gave him his customary above the head finger wave.

Shryer mouthed the words, *you're welcome!*

***

Her arrows found shaytan throats and joints with surgical precision as she moved through the corridor.

A shaytan commander staggered backward.

"You serve Desatyr!" he said as he fell back, unconscious.

Shanna then morphed into Kalgorie.

"I serve Convergence!" He replied coldly. "You are over," he said as he morphed into a large black panther and started moving further through the ship.

***

Elsewhere inside the ship, Nirvana and Shryer cleared a hangar bay as a large metal door hissed while sliding open, revealing a host of armed shaytans who looked in at their brethren lying unconscious on the floor.

For the first time since the invasion began, shaytans retreated.

Hope flickered.

Nirvana smiled at Shryer as without warning a kick sent her flying against a wall.

Her head smacked against it and she fell unconscious.

He then swung hard and knocked Shryer out.

He huffed. "Cheap magician!"

He then growled as he looked down at two of the unconscious guards. "Put them in a holding cell," he barked.

"Yes my lord!" proclaimed the shaytans who were entering the area with him.

CHAPTER TWENTY-TWO

DESATYR MOVED STEADILY, angrily through the halls of the warship, stepping over the bodies of unconscious or completely fallen shaytans.

He did not roar.

He did not rush.

He simply walked.

A blue blur moved towards him and he simply stuck his foot out in a zip movement, catching the speedy youth by surprise.

Altimari heard the crack in his foot as he stumbled and slammed uncontrollably into a wall.

He crashed so hard that he heard some bones crack as he fell to the floor.

"Collect him," Desatyr simply said as he kept walking.

He soon came to his fallen bridge and looked around as a shaytan approached him.

"Has word come back from the rest of my fleet?" he asked.

"Not as of yet Desatyr," replied the shaytan as Desatyrs' eyes shifted around the room before he quickly picked up the shaytan by the collar and held him up just above his own head.

"You spent all that time on my ship and never once realized my soldiers never address me by name?"

The shaytan looked down at him as Desatyr just threw him across the bridge.

The shaytan then morphed into the black panther where his paws met the wall and he leapt back in the direction of Desatyr.

Desatyr poised himself in position, ready to catch the black panther.

The black panther quickly morphed into a large gray rhino and landed on Desatyr whose scream was muffled by the large mass of the Rhino.

Kalgorie as the rhino snorted and smiled. "How's that for realization?"

The rhino then welched and bent his head forward as he heard a tear, followed by successive multiple tears as blood spewed from his mouth as the giant shaytan pushed the rhino up into the ceiling where he hit it and morphed back into his human form before falling and hitting the floor as Desatyr quickly rolled up with his bloody dagger in hand!"

"COLLECT HIM!" he yelled as two shaytans quickly moved Kalgories' body.

Desatyr snarled. "One more...where are you?"

She screamed angrily as she came at him, moving flawlessly, strength, foresight, speed in harmony.

She appeared before him and grabbed his arm and slammed him downward, using her knee to catch his face.

She drew a sword of golden light and nearly drove her blade into his chest, but Desatyr caught her wrist.

"You misunderstand," he said quietly. "The orb didn't just reshape my non shaytan generals...it didn't just make me ...emperor, I exploited it for personal gain, and that permanent gain has made me what I am!"

A flashback.

A regular looking shaytan, decades ago, stumbled across the vitos orb. It tried to teach him, shape him, mold him into a good leader for his kind. But the information he learned from the orb would make him hunger for power.

His form shifted slightly.

He grew taller.

He became sharper.

His sills became more refined.

The flashback ended.

"The orb had hoped that I would become an anchor. To be a part of what Sorrie and Chrystal are as Convergence. but I had a different path in mind. So I took ownership."

The revelation landed like a blow.

"That is why I am not merely stronger," he said. "I am evolved."

He struck her and she flew involuntarily across the bridge where she crashed into a wall.

She raised her hand as he moved towards her. *Sleep,* she thought as she rose again.

"I'm not tired," he said as he punched her in the face.

Cherokee fell unconscious.

Desatyr then looked around and saw Gaylor's body.

He sighed as he then turned to an approaching shaytan. "Take this one and put her on the same row as the others!"

"Yes my lord," said the shaytan as he immediately called two of his comrades over to help him with her body."

Desatyr continued to scan the bridge. "Looks like I got the whole set," he said.

CHAPTER TWENTY-THREE

EVEN WITH THE shaytans moving through the halls past the cells, seemingly not at all impressed they were captured, the area was still and quiet.

There was no screaming.

There was no rage.

There was only an understanding and realization that they were clearly outmatched.

The whole time they had been fighting this war, Desatyr kept his best and most efficient hand hidden under the advisement of the orb, himself.

He basked in the cockiness of his almost flawless victory as he directed his shaytans to the task of cleaning up the dead and repairing the ship.

Maybe, he thought, *I don't have to abandon my plans with this planet after all.*

He would find the treacherous, ungrateful wench, Shanna, as well as the lanky Vael, and dispose of them properly.

The inhabitants of this planet will surely meet their demise.

***

Cherokee stirred first. She painfully sat up and looked through the intentionally fashioned translucent cells and saw her fallen Guards of Telari

She closed her eyes,

Convergence appeared as a green light moving about in the vast darkness of her field of vision.

Cherokee didn't sob. She expressed no sign of weakness. But she did feel guilt and regret and that essence became apparent to Convergence.

"I am sorry Convergence," she started. "I have failed the people of Telari. I have failed the other Guards. I have failed you."

"Have you now?" asked Convergence. "I don't think your destiny has quite been fulfilled."

Cherokee laughed sarcastically. "Destiny? Look at us! He took us all out by being faster, stronger, more cunning, wittier, ..."

"...than each of you could be," interrupted Convergence. "You have always known that beating him wasn't going..."

"...to take one of us," interrupted Cherokee. "It would take all of us."

"You know what must be done," Convergence said gently.

"Yes, but one guard alone cannot survive that type of synergy," said Cherokee.

"Survival of one guard is not the key," replied Convergence. "Survival of a people is the goal!"

Cherokee realized that in leading The Guards of Telari, she became the one weapon that would unify them and save the planet as well as everything in between.

She recognized that as this were to be her destiny, her time had come.

"Thank you, Convergence," she relented.

"You are welcome our sister!"

From the broken bodies of her four comrades, the medallions emerged from their torsos which healed them all immediately.

The images of the medallions made their way to Cherokees' cell as Nicole, Alex, Steve, and Kevin looked on.

Cherokees' medallion soon emerged from her chest, changing her back into Christina.

It then merged with the other four medallions, making it difficult to completely discern one image from the next.

The large medallion soon flipped over and over again into Christina's direction while growing in size, until it swung over her head completely until she was no longer Christina.

She didn't quite look like Cherokee either.

She stood before them looking imposing and stronger than she looked previously.

The gold chest plating was the same as was her mask and cape, but she had a multitude of colors that swirled around her; beneath the gold armor of her legs were swirls of blue and purple, and around her arms were swirls of red and green below her gold plating where it used to be black.

Behind her mask where her eyes normally sat was a red light. And her hair was now fixed in locks which afforded her greater control.

Cherokee looked behind her at the guards. "Alex, Nicole, Kevin, and Steve, you four have been through enough. I will finish this fight. It is best if I keep you here to ensure your safety.

They all protested.

"This is over! she said as she flew out of the cell without movement of door.

CHAPTER TWENTY-FOUR

AS THE MIGHTY warship started to elevate again, Desatyr turned his head in the direction of the sound of a loud crash.

"What was that noise?" he asked angrily as Cherokee flew effortlessly through the metal wall.

"There you go she said," as she quickly ran into Desatyr and grabbed a hold of him. She pulled up and flew the two of them directly out of the ship.

Once outside and up in the air she flipped them over so that he was facing her with his back toward the ground and she punched him so hard and fast that he crashed down and skid into the ground making him look like a meteorite which had just crashed.

The sky above Telari became fractured as red lightening split the sky.

Not broken.

Fractured.

The shaytan warship loomed overhead like a wound in the heavens, its underbelly pulsing with unstable light as the charging of the molecular decomposition cannon hummed halfway towards completion.

Desatyr stood up groggily as he was caught off guard by the tackle.

He looked up at Cherokee and smiled. "You look different! I imagine once I take control of you, you'd make a trophy bride."

"Don't flatter yourself!" Cherokee replied. "Any marriage you have at this point will be to the afterlife!"

Desatyr growled and then jumped up angrily at Cherokee.

As he approached her, he reached for her neck and clasped his hands, shocked that she wasn't there as she grabbed his collar from behind and threw him back towards the ground.

She then sped down past him in a blue gold blur and kicked him causing him to fly back upward as he heard some of his own bones crack.

As he flew upward, a doorway opened up and he flew into it.

The doorway spit him out just above ground and right in front of Cherokee.

Desatyr looked up at her.

The gold chest plating gleamed as it always had. The mask remained, regal, unyielding, her cape flowing behind her in disciplined arcs.

She was no longer the singular leader of The Guards of Telari.

Beneath the gold armor of her legs, swirls of blue and purple coursed like living rivers. Around her arms, red and green spiraled beneath her plating where black once lay dormant.

All the changes observed by her guards, he now saw.

"You dare attempt to combine what was meant to be divided?" he asked weakly.

Cherokee's voice answered layered, five tones in one.

"I do not combine," she said. "I converge."

He growled.

She picked him up.

Her fist struck his jaw with Nirvana's strength behind it.

The impact cracked the air.

Desatyr flew backward through several trees, which snapped instantly like twigs, leaving their stumps behind, partially uprooted due to the pull of his impact.

He rose immediately and spat what looked to be blood down to his left side.

He moved faster towards her.

He then lunged.

Cherokee did not dodge.

Like an iron wall, she absorbed the blow.

Invincible.

He fell back.

Nirvana's durability, tenfold surged through her.

Desatyr's strike, one that would have shattered bones in any other mortal, merely rippled across her armor in waves of gold.

Cherokee extended her hand.

Light geometry formed mid-air, intricate sigils layered in impossible symmetry.

Metal screamed as the distortion tore through the molecular decomposition cannon, shutting it down.

Desatyr roared now.

"I told you," he growled. "I am unstoppable!"

He blurred forward, faster than any shaytan should be capable.

Cherokee met him in mid-air.

Speed against speed.

Blow against blow.

The sky filled with streaks of blue-gold and red as they collided faster than sight could perceive.

Desatyr finally caught her by the throat.

Lifted her high.

"You cannot sustain this," he said quietly. "Five guards in one vessel. You will burn."

Cherokee smiled beneath her mask.

Then she changed.

Her form rippled.

Gold plating shifted into sinew.

Armor into fur.

She became massive.

A silverback gorilla, Kalgories' primal strength unleashed.

Her arms wrapped around Desatyr's torso.

She slammed him downward.

The impact split the battlefield.

Before he could recover, she shifted again, wolf bit his right arm, eagle pecked him in his left eye, serpent wrapped around his fist and neck and caused him to punch himself. The forms flowing one into another with impossible grace.

She struck from every angle.

Every instinct sharpened.

Every predator awakened.

Desatyr tore free and blasted her with a beam of concentrated void.

Cherokee answered with Shryer's mystic shield layered with Nirvana's invulnerability.

The void fractured against her like glass against granite.

The sky began to collapse around them.

The warship trembled.

Desatyr grew desperate.

He gathered all his power into one strike, a final, annihilating pulse meant to atomize her entirely.

Cherokee did not evade.

She closed her eyes.

She reached inward.

To speed. To strength. To mind. To magic. To instinct.

Then she exhaled.

All five energies ignited at once.

She became light.

Not blinding.

Unified.

She drove forward, through his attack, through his defenses, through his superiority.

Her hand pierced his chest.

Gold and red collided.

Desatyr screamed.

Not in pain.

In disbelief.

"You were meant to fall before me alone!"
he roared.

"We were meant to unite as one," she
replied.

She unleashed everything.

The magic from all five medallions burned
through her veins and into him.

Desatyr's evolved form began to crack.

Not crumble.

Crack.

Fractures of red light split across his frame.

He tried to resist.

Tried to dominate.

Tried to expand.

But unity does not splinter.

It converges.

With a final cry that shook the warship in
the sky itself,

Desatyr shattered into ash and fading
crimson vapor.

The sky cleared.

The warship's hum faltered.

Shaytan warriors froze.

Then fled.

The cannon dead.

Cherokee hovered alone above the
battlefield.

The swirls of color around her dimmed.

The red light behind her mask softened.

She descended slowly.

Gracefully.

The ground met her feet.

The wind stilled.

The five energies flickered once more, then began to fade.

She used the magic to create a rectangular doorway.

Alex, Nicole, Steve, and Kevin all emerged from the doorway, and it closed behind them.

They all ran up to Cherokee and wrapped their arms around her.

"It is finally done," she said.

CHAPTER TWENTY-FIVE

THE BATTLEFIELD WAS quiet as the shaytan warship now sat on the ground, seeming quiet and lifeless.

Cherokee stood with her guards.

"It is time that I return your medallions to you," she said.

"You have to let me try that one day," started Nicole excitedly, "all that power!"

"The medallions," started Cherokee, "are not meant to be housed in one vessel. The use of such raw power in such a way will only tear the body away atom by atom."

"Wait...what?" asked Altimari.

"But you had them within you?" queried Steve.

"I did," Cherokee said, "it was a necessary last resort to save our world, and our people."

"You knew this would happen?" asked Nicole, "and you did it anyway?"

"This was not a decision I made lightly," started Cherokee, "I consulted with Convergence before I made such a decision."

"There...there's gotta be something we can do," protested Steve. "I can do a healing spell as soon as we have our medallions back."

"It does not work that way," replied Cherokee.

"Well, just keep the stupid medallions," cried Nicole. we don't need them anyway."

"The body cannot maintain this way," said Cherokee. "Do not be sad, this was always my destiny, to take my place as the third Trinity and complete the Convergence."

"Wait, you are Convergence?" asked Kevin.

"I am of Convergence," said Cherokee.

The Guards knelt around her.

Then,

Light gathered.

Her form rose, luminous and gentle.

"Always remember your path," she said softly. "You are the Guards of Telari now!"

"What'll we do without a leader?"

She smiled at each of them.

"You are all capable of leading, but I do have a plan for future guidance."

Cherokee glowed brighter.

And as the guards looked around, the scenery darkened.

They were back in Mount Sinovian.

A tear came to Steve's eye, as he watched as his lifelong best friend started to slowly ascend upwards.

"Are you sure there isn't another way," cried Nicole.

"You are ready now," she said as she slowly ascended up into the darkness in red light.

The medallions materialized on the canyon floor below them.

They each reached down and picked up their medallion and there was a fifth one on the floor.

Steve picked up the medallion. "Who is this for?" he asked.

The symbol was a perfect circle with a radiant star in the center. There were subtle flares about the circle.

"You will take the shaytan warship and deliver the remaining shaytans to their home world. Any prisoners still on board are welcome to stay on Telari or you can drop them off to any suitable planet on your way."

"On our way where?" asked Alex.

"To your home world of origin," replied Convergence. "Shryer's magic can guide the ship which will be powerful enough to get you there and back safely."

The medallion will lead you to the one who will now be tasked with leading you."

Nicole and Kevin looked at each other.

"I guess we get to take that trip after all," said Kevin.

"What was that?" asked Alex.

Shryer put a hand on his shoulder. "I'll explain it to you at a later time."

"For the Trinity, for Telari!" they proclaimed in unison.

Four medallions flipped forward growing in size and then flipped back over them changing them into the remaining four Guards of Telari.

They stood together in unity.

They stood together with shared strength.

They stood as one.

EPILOGUE

THE GOLDEN LION ran down Academy Road in Northeast Philadelphia as cars screeched out of way and as people screamed in an attempt to move out of its way.

The sky was darkened and people in the area just couldn't believe what they were seeing.

The lion then saw some trees to the left of Woodhaven Road and darted in that direction with the hopes of finding some temporary solace as he pressed forward with his mission.

The air was cool, the sky a midnight blue, unlike his home world, which had a hue of light green.

The domicile units also seemed to be much more complex than that of Telari.

"Kalgorie," started Altimari over a transmitter in the cats' ear, "where are you?"

"I am hidden in some trees," started Kalgorie as he huffed and puffed. "I don't understand, I came in this form because I heard humans liked lions."

"You are in the wrong country my friend," started Altimari, "in this location they like dogs and cats!"

"Really?" asked Kalgorie. "That's so lame!"

Kalgorie was soon distracted by a purple glow coming from behind him, causing him to turn around.

"Easy there big fella ," started Gemini as she lowered herself to the ground while in her pure energy form, glowing a bright purple, just in case the big cat came at her.

"I think...I think I found her!" exclaimed Kalgorie, catching Gemini by surprise. Converge on my coordinates!"

"You can talk?" asked Gemini as her body stopped glowing.

Kalgorie looked at himself. "Oh, my apologies..." He said as he then morphed into his Telarian form.

"I am Kalgorie...are you April? April Jenkins?"

Gemini looked around nervously. "Please don't say my name so loud like that, "I have an identity to keep protected."

Kalgorie looked downward. "Secret identity, right," he started nervously. "I am Kalgorie from the planet Telari. "We were sent to ask you to come to Telari to lead us."

"We?" asked Gemini.

A doorway appeared near the pair and Shryer, Nirvana, and Altimari all walked out,

"We are The Guards of Telari!"

Shryer stepped forward and handed her a medallion.

"We were sent here to seek your leadership in the ongoing protection of our home world, Telari."

Gemini looked at the small group and then at the medallion Shryer had passed to her.

"Huh!" she said.

About the Author

Derrick J. Truesdale is a healthcare professional who spent over thirty years wanting to tell the stories he believed would both entertain and inspire. Today, those long-held ideas have become interconnected science fiction and fantasy novels that stand alone while forming a larger, evolving universe.

His worlds can be dark at times—but they are never without purpose. He writes with the hope of encouraging others to explore their imagination, embrace transformation, and discover strength in unexpected places.

Welcome to the world of Semaj, where seemingly separate stories share deeper connections waiting to be discovered

www.SemajBooks.com.